All the Conspirators

CHRISTOPHER ISHERWOOD

a novel

All the Conspirators

A NEW DIRECTIONS BOOK

Library of Congress Catalog Card Number: 58-12798

Manufactured in the United States of America
First published clothbound (ISBN: 0-8112-0293-3) in 1958 and as
New Directions Paperbook 480 (ISBN: 0-8112-0725-0) in 1979

New Directions Books are published for James Laughlin
by New Directions Publishing Corporation,
80 Eighth Avenue, New York 10011

To
EDWARD UPWARD

FOREWORD

A cormorant, startling them with its queer cry, broke flapping from unseen rocks below and vanished into the empty gulf of light westward, like an absurd impulse of desperation, towards America.

IT amuses me to regard the above sentence — the last of the first chapter of this novel — as an unconscious prophecy. Nearly twenty years ago, its author with his queer cry flapped his way across the Atlantic. His eldest book now belatedly follows him and comes to roost for the first time in America, beside some of its younger brothers on the friendly perch of New Directions.

I started writing *All the Conspirators* in the spring of 1926, when I was twenty-one years old. Two years later, after rejections and revisions, it was published in London by Jonathan Cape. If you should care to read about its origins I must refer you to my autobiography, *Lions and Shadows.*

Cyril Connolly, in his brilliant but too generous introduction to Cape's 1939 reissue of this novel in their Travellers' Library series, writes politely of its author's 'austere and conscientious assumption of a co-operative and intelligent reader'. If you flatter yourself that you are co-operative and intelligent, see what you can make of, for example, the first three and a half pages of the last chapter! I now detect a great deal of repressed aggression in this kind of obscurity. Young writers are apt to employ it as a secret language which is intelligible only to members of their group. Outsiders are thereby challenged to admit that they don't understand it or dared to pretend that they do — to be unmasked in any case, sooner or later, as squares.

My instinctive use of this modern epithet — for which I can't even think of an earlier equivalent — makes me ask myself: could the author of this novel conceivably be described as a prehistoric Angry Young Man? Well — as a young man, he was certainly angry — God help us if the time ever comes when young men aren't — but his anger had a different frame of reference. Today's Angry Young Man (who will curse me for using that silly but convenient label once again) is angry with Society and its official representatives; he calls them hypocrites, he challenges the truth of what they teach. He declares that a social revolution has taken place of which they are trying to remain unaware. He accuses them of reactionary dullness, snobbery, complacency, apathy. While they mouth their platitudes, he exclaims, we are all drifting toward nuclear war.

The Angry Young Man of my generation was angry with the Family and its official representatives; he called them hypocrites, he challenged the truth of what they taught. He declared that a Freudian revolution had taken place of which they were trying to remain unaware. He accused them of reactionary dullness, snobbery, complacency, apathy. While they mouthed their platitudes, he exclaimed, we were all drifting toward mental disease, sex crime, alcoholism, suicide.

Nevertheless, there is always an emotional solidarity between rebels. And if the Allen Chalmers of my story could have been taken to see John Osborne's plays he would have been sympathetically thrilled by their anger, just as I am in my middle age today.

All the Conspirators may be regarded as a very very late Victorian novel, for it recalls the days when parents were still heavies. It records a minor engagement in what Shelley calls 'the great war between the old and young'. And what a war that was! Every battle of it was fought to a finish, with no quarter asked or shown. The vanquished became love-starved old maids, taciturn bitter bachelors, chronic invalids, harmless lunatics; or they died, if they were lucky. You may call the motives of these characters trivial, but their struggle is mortal and passionate. And the author is as passionate as any of his characters. He makes not the smallest pretence of impartiality. His battle-cry is 'My Generation — right or wrong!'

Perhaps you will be able to enjoy this book simply as a period piece — smiling at its naive attempts at a James Joyce thought-stream, its aping of the mannerisms of Stephen Dedalus, its quaint echoes of Virginia Woolf, its jerky flashback narration crudely imitated from E. M. Forster. But even if this were now its only interest, there would still be one thing about it which hadn't dated, as far as I was concerned; its dedication. After half a lifetime, Edward Upward is still the friend he has always been; still the judge before whom all my work must stand trial and from whose verdict, much as I sometimes hate to admit it, there is no appeal.

I now extend my dedication to include Edward's wife Hilda, their daughter Kathy and their son Christopher.

C. I.

July 1958

ALL THE CONSPIRATORS

CHAPTER I

'ALL the time the wind was south-west you were deadly keen on seals.'

'Was I?' Allen idly stopped fumbling in the pocket of his coat, then asked with interest: 'Been seeing your friend the boatman again?'

'Yes. Why?'

'This meteorological knowledge.'

'I suppose you think I'm incapable of noticing anything for myself.'

'No.'

There were blue fishing-boats in the harbour pool. Allen could see them reflected in blots of opaque colour on the glass of a framed engraving which faced the window. Sir Cloud-esley Shovel and his men drowning between the Gilstone and Retarriers, 1707. The blots did not seem to move, but the fishing-boats were dipping and rocking as gusts darkened the water. A web of fragile brilliance lay upon the pool and upon the distant waters of the Road. The dining-room was shadowy with reflected light.

'I can actually remember your saying: "at the

Zoo they'll answer to obscene names : Milly and Gertie.' "

'The seals aren't the point,' replied Allen, beginning to clean his pipe.

Philip asked: 'Then what is?' merely to keep up the discussion. Like a becalmed kite, it required continual jerks. Another argument occurred to him.

'There'd be eight of us in the launch.'

'Nine,' Allen corrected, 'including the boatman.'

'Well, then?'

'What?'

The light played over Philip's face, which was beginning to peel. Sunburn made it agreeable, almost handsome. But against the dark blue sky and the rakish mop-headed palms of the hotel garden, Philip, in his townish clothes, looked plump and rather absurd. Or one could put it that, behind him, the gorgeous colours of the afternoon beyond the pane seemed crude, unreal. He was smiling with exasperation.

'Well, then, what earthly difference can it make?'

'None.'

'Then you'll come?'

'No.'

'But, if it doesn't, why won't you?'

'Because I don't want to.' Allen yawned patiently.

'Rot. If you don't come, it's because of him.'

'Just as you like. It's because of him.'

Philip sighed; saying with a certain pathos:

'Oh, Allen, you are utterly impossible some-times, you know.'

They were alone in the dining-room. The other visitors had either finished their meal already or were off for the day picnicking on one of the smaller islands. Within the house there was no sound. The tide was in, the waves splashing in sharp slaps against the terrace wall. On the gravel, the gulls were jostling like hens for the scraps of food scattered by the waiter. A gust gave a whip-crack to the rope of the green flagstaff. The breeze was freshening.

'In twenty minutes they'll have started.'

Allen finished cleaning his pipe, filled it carefully, lit it, puffed. Then he said:

'But why should this stop your going?'

'Oh, I shall go, of course. Don't flatter yourself.'

Allen watched through the window a tall young man in light brown tweeds come hurriedly into view round the angle of the hotel buildings. He was fair-haired, childishly pink. He frowned. There was nobody else on the terrace.

'Colonel Page won't be there, you know,'

13

Philip added. 'He went off early this morning to the western rocks.'

'I wonder,' said Allen, watching, 'whether the desire to photograph puffins during the love act could be classified as any form of sexual mania.'

'It ought. It's lasted for twenty years.'

The young man, frowning anxiously, had disappeared.

'I'm going,' said Allen, rising abruptly.

'Where?'

'Oh, anywhere. Out of this house, for the present.'

'You aren't going to explain to him or anything?'

'I'll explain whatever you like, if you tell me what to say.'

'Explain why we ever came to this place at all,' thought Philip, angry for a moment.

An ordnance map spread out under the lamplight on the tablecloth in Allen's lodgings. Menavawr. Inisvowels. Nornor. Ganilly. Hanjague. Miles and miles out in the Atlantic. Absolutely no question of meeting anyone. They'll never guess. A poster seen in the Warren Street tube station had released sensory and motor images of gulls, passing, repassing. And from the greasy filth of Paddington goods siding one false overpowering breath of rotten seaweed. My God, how utterly terrific. The Franck Symphony contributed three bars. A Saint-Blaise, à la Zuecca. Can't we start *now*?

'Oh, it doesn't matter. Page ought to understand you if anybody does.'

As they passed together from the dining-room into the faded sunlit lounge, Allen experienced a pang of boredom which was like hunger or love, curdling the food in his stomach, making him feel helpless and physically sick.

.   .   .   .   .   .

Down the smuggler's alley, high-walled, overgrown with dangling fuschia, they idly strolled, by a path which led to the cliff. Cottages, limewashed or crude pink in the ocean sunlight, surrounded a stony foreshore littered with empty tins, vegetables, smashed baskets and mouldering boots. Their threads of smoke curled up faintly against the sea-line. The fields beyond were full of wallflowers and shrivelled daffodils. Two donkeys were coupling with a loud monotonous braying which echoed from the rocks.

'You'll miss the launch,' said Allen.

'Well, you don't really expect me to go alone, do you?'

'I can't see why not.'

'For one thing, I'm not specially keen to, now. Other people,' Philip smiled maliciously, 'are allowed to change their minds.'

Allen did not reply. 'I've been fairly asking for it, all through lunch,' he thought. 'All the same, it's unfortunate, because if we're together all this afternoon we shall certainly have a row.'

But Philip had, as it happened, at that moment seen a picture. Squinted at for an instant with half-closed eyelids, Morning Point, Peninnis and an intervening segment of the Atlantic had all at once composed into a very striking arrangement of interlocked triangles. The effect suggested an agreeable line of treatment. Colour laid on with the palette-knife or smeared in with one's thumb. A few hours' work; bold, attractive, easy. In his excitement he unwisely began trying to explain the idea to Allen.

'You quite follow?'

'I think so. Just blue and green and grey.'

'You mean you think it's obvious?'

'Oh, no. Not obvious, certainly.'

'Well then, what's wrong with it?'

'I never said anything was wrong. As a matter of fact, I can't possibly tell until I've seen what you make of it.'

'No, of course you can't. That's the worst of

your not understanding the thing practically.
You have to judge it from a purely literary point
of view.'

Allen was thinking: 'Now, I won't be the one
to start this. It would be too ignominious to lose
one's temper over Philip's daubs.'

He said:

'What about your view of the harbour?'

'Oh, that, naturally, I shall scrap.'

'What's the matter with it all of a sudden?'

'I must say, I should have thought *anyone* could
have seen.'

'You mean that the drawing's all wrong?'
[Why am I so spiteful today?] 'But seriously,
Philip, I did like that thing.'

'You know, Allen,' Philip's tone softened a
little, 'for an intelligent person you've got the
worst taste of anybody I ever met.'

'Have I? I dare say. But from "a purely
literary point of view" it appealed to me. It was
so extraordinarily, well – interesting. The huge
empty foreground and those boats like collapsed
tents. And then the stone pier looking as if it
was glued on to the islands beyond, without any
attempt to suggest distance at all. It reminded me
of that picture by Matisse.'

But this speech, to judge from a side-glance at

Philip's face, had been altogether tactless. Allen added rather weakly:

'Or perhaps it isn't Matisse.'

'I suppose,' Philip was peevish again, 'you've made up your mind that this new thing isn't going to be "interesting."'

Further concession would be mere insult.

'Not *so* interesting,' said Allen firmly.

'I thought not. You see it's just this unfortunate craving for the bizarre which handicaps you, every time. What you call interesting is so often merely quaint, or worse.'

'And what *you* call interesting, is?' Allen had begun grinning provokingly, in spite of himself. Philip seeing it, grinned also, but his self-satirical tone was strained:

'Well, I must say — without being too personal — that I do think I've got an enthusiasm for, one might call them, more *genuine* forms of life. I rather prefer to tackle the subjects that you think — though you don't seem to have got the honesty to admit it — obvious; and extract something from *them*. It's easy enough to be "interesting" in your way.'

'And these "genuine forms of life" that you extract things from, include?'

'Oh, if you want a catalogue — well, put it that

I'm not *afraid* of anything. One's got to have the nerve. I want to do picture-postcard sunsets, cows crossing a stream, yes, and hunting scenes, children making daisy-chains, a cat with her kittens. . .'

'And boatmen?'

That had done it.

'Yes, boatmen. As a matter of fact, that's a particularly apt example. Because one of the worst consequences of your attitude is that it makes you so impossibly snobbish. Anyone whom you suspect of the ghastly crime of being ordinary is, of course, utterly beneath your notice.'

'Utterly.'

From the headland they overlooked quivering sheets of intense light, dotted with black lumps, like worms-cast on a smooth lawn, the Western Rocks. On one of these rocks knelt Colonel Page, cramped in his cache of stones, peering forward through a chink, breathing heavily and gripping the pipe between his teeth in his excitement, as his hairy fingers toyed with the rubber bulb of the camera shutter. Peninnis stands amidst its own enormous ruins; clumsy smooth shapes of protean aspect, at different angles, to different eyes. One sees there the winged horse and the gorgon, molars or fists of giants, a temple's architrave,

19

heads of nubians and of pythons thrust from beneath immense burdens of stone; thigh, torso,
buttocks, limbs, phallic symbols male and
female. About fifty yards from the shore, the
curded foam was bubbling over a huge slab,
channelled deeply by the tides. Philip had noticed
it on their first walk here, the day of their arrival.
'I say, Allen, isn't that absolutely Epstein? Do
you see, three corpses, and the centre one has got
its stomach eaten out by rats?'

'If you did any kind of creative work you'd soon
learn that one's own point of view *isn't enough*.
You've got also to look at things in the way that
your so-called uninteresting and ordinary people
look at them.'

'Very well, then,' Allen roused himself. The
strong air was making him yawn. 'How would an
ordinary person look at that rock?'

'In the first place,' began Philip, with great
deliberation, 'it's obviously quite impossible for
me to answer that question unless I know a good
deal more about the kind of "ordinary" person
to which you're referring. Your definitions are so
delightfully vague and arbitrary.'

Holding a match to his pipe, Allen thought:
'Shall I?'

'All right. Take Victor Page.'

Philip frowned. Then he said coldly:

'Very well.'

Allen watched him, grinning.

'Come along. How would he?'

'I suppose you think it's immensely funny to drag Page's name in on all occasions. Some people wouldn't harp on it quite so much, considering – '

'You mean that you haven't the slightest idea. Well, I'll tell you. He'd look at it and say that it was a rock. A big rock. Now. How does that help you?'

Frowning, Philip sat down on a boulder.

'I must say this, Allen – since you insist on discussing him – that I only hope Page understands your childish behaviour as well as I do. At breakfast it was damnable.'

'What did I do at breakfast? Well, we'd always had separate tables before. And if you can be civil to him and his uncle during a whole meal, well, I can't.'

Philip sighed.

'I simply give you up. One would think it was a mortal offence to have been at school with you.'

'I do wish you could get it clear in your head that, at school, we were in different houses. I barely knew him.'

'Oh, very well then. I only know that he nearly pulled your arm off when we first ran into them on the pier.'

'My dear Philip, don't the old boys of your school – ? Oh, of course, I forgot. But imagine the effect. Landing from a steamer. In a place like this. The nervous shock would be considerable. The rest was pure tribal emotion.'

'It's easy enough to sneer at people whose impulses aren't always negative.'

This, from Philip, was surprisingly acute. Allen, stung for a moment, replied with heat:

'Even with your latest theories, I suppose you'll hardly be hypocrite enough to pretend that Page doesn't loathe me as much as I loathe him?'

'At least he can be decently civil.'

'Haven't I been?'

'Well, in a beastly way. I can see all sorts of meanings in the things you say to him. Probably he's much more sensitive than you think.'

'And I can see all sorts of meanings in the things he says to me. You study him a bit more closely, Philip. Remember, you've got to get thoroughly at his point of view.'

Philip drew in a deep breath, rather ostentatiously biting his lips.

'Every day, each time we meet, there's some unpleasantness in the air. Look at this afternoon. It's getting intolerable.'

'Quite. Well, what do you suggest we do?'

'I must say, I should have thought it was for you to suggest something.'

Again Allen lit his pipe; this time, as it seemed to Philip, with deliberate slowness.

'Go back to London,' he said at last.

'Do be reasonable.'

'You've heard nothing yet?'

'Is it likely?'

Philip rose to his feet, stretching himself wearily: posture of bored crucifixion, against the sea.

'I thought Joan would have written.'

'To treat me to mother's comments? No. She'd spare me those.'

'She'll let you know when things have calmed down.'

'If they do.' Philip yawned and sighed. 'I sometimes wonder whether one'll ever go back to that house.'

'What if you don't?'

'God knows. Clear out abroad, I suppose.'

Down at the harbour, Allen had read the names of the tramps at their moorings – *Young Ernie*.

Justifier. Realize. United Friends. They had
watched the fair-haired boy from the Danish
timber vessel strolling with three girls under the
palisades of the ruined fort, rust-bitten by the
spray. He had picked off sharp flakes of iron with
his fingers, and the girls laughed. Philip in sea-
boots on Havre quay, beneath shuttered houses
and the windows from which bolsters limply
hang.

'You were an utter lunatic,' said Allen, with a
half-admiring grin.

Their mood brightened.

'I wonder when I really decided to do it.'

'You certainly fixed things up pretty quickly.'

'I believe it was after that ghastly tea-party of
mother's; when Currants asked me in front of
those two hags when I was going to get something into the Academy.'

'Did she really? You never told me that.'

'My God, that's nothing. It wasn't worth
mentioning. The only wonder is I stuck the whole
show as long as I did.'

Their pleased smiles slowly shrank. Allen
kicked a pebble with his heel. Philip's voice was
peevish again:

'And meanwhile?'

'Meanwhile, what?'

'How are we going to carry on here?'

Allen said good-naturedly:

'Oh, I suppose I'll do my best.'

'After all,' he was thinking, 'Philip's got himself into rather a hole, and certainly I've helped him there. And if Page and I have a row, he suffers for it. Properly appreciated, Philip's a martyr – of sorts.'

'Only don't expect too much,' he added.

'I knew you'd see it like that.' Philip was, as usual, mistakenly touched by the suddenness of Allen's softenings – or weakenings. He was eagerly conciliatory:

'Mind you, Allen, I absolutely understand your point of view.'

Well, to a certain extent they had had it out, and perhaps the situation was easier. They had, at least, not quite quarrelled. And already, as they began to descend the path, Philip was contentedly launched into a fresh explanation of his picture-to-be. 'I shall do five or six right off now that I've started. I feel I've got the hang of this place at last. And if we do go back to town there's certain to be one of those newspaper stunts on. They do it for advertisement, you know. You send you stuff up, and if they like it, it gets hung in their show. It wouldn't be so bad for a beginning. And I think it'd make a great impression in the home, don't you? At any rate, it would show mother that I mean business. If only she'd get that much clear.'

'You might write some more poetry too, don't you think?'

Allen thought:

'How strange. I said that in the sort of tone one uses to a child.'

The crescent of the harbour rose into view. 'Yes, it's funny you should ask, because only this morning I had the really brilliant idea of combining those two old things about the gulls at Vauxhall Bridge. With a new one. You see the contrast.'

Allen nodded seriously. 'But I only caught bits of what he was saying. I must get into the habit of listening carefully. It distracts the mind. Since I've been here, I've done far too much thinking.'

The pretty little buildings along the shore. Rat Island. The boats. The sparkling water. Again that slight sharp qualm of nausea, just under the plexus. Boredom belongs to the group of cancerous diseases. Can I stand this for another whole fortnight?

A cormorant, startling them with its queer cry,

ALL THE CONSPIRATORS
broke flapping from unseen rocks below and
vanished into the empty gulf of light westward,
like an absurd impulse of desperation, towards
America.

CHAPTER II

COLONEL Page was a very tall man. The sun had burnt his body sallow like pig-skin and his knees were covered with black freckles. His hands trembled. He used brilliantine for his thin, dark hair, and during the daytime wore a service wrist-watch, tweed jacket, brogues, stockings with tabs and khaki shorts. In a house built of plaster, tree branches and grass, at the edge of a bamboo forest, he had formed the habit of dressing regularly for dinner.

'You cut in and feed, Victor. I won't be two shakes.'

'No, sir. I'd rather wait.'

At their small corner table, watched by the eleven other visitors to the hotel, they conversed briefly, facing each other, in deep quiet tones. Victor wore a single-knot bow tie; his uncle the old straight kind. Both were washed like school-boys. Colonel Page's neck looked as though his collar hurt him. Whenever he had spoken, he touched his small moustache with the napkin.

By the lake Naivasha he has seen pin-tail, English garganey. And on Norfolk Broads, from a punt, late at dawn. Has woken to feel the weight across the blanket of heavy coils. Lie stone-still;

28

then kick out and jump for your life. At Limerick, regimental cricket, bird-nesting in Shannon Woods; after Church Parade the band plays in the barrack square. Verdi, by request. Short-fused, at Hell Corner, a jam-pot grenade bursting too soon crippled his well-known action, ugly, left-handed.

'Yes. My uncle's knocked about a good deal.'

Afterwards, in the lounge, they took out their pipes. Colonel Page's was short and heavy; Victor's slender, with a flattened bowl. Colonel Page's tobacco pouch was made of cheap black rubber.

'Have some of mine, sir?'

'Thanks. I will. I get sickened to death of this stuff.'

Grateful, Victor gave his uncle a light, inhaled with a small earnest frown. At something, he uttered two laughs. Ha-ha. Ha-ha-ha. His glance crossed the room, met the eyes of a girl who listened. Back it telescoped. He flushed, myopic.

But what did they talk about? Once Allen had heard Colonel Page say:

'The Hun did me a personal favour by mopping up the last two of 'em on the Somme.'

.   .   .   .   .   .

At nine, or earlier, he went upstairs.

Victor hated this moment. The three girls were watching him, candidly. In the daytime, if he met one or other of them, he smiled, said something cheerful, quite at ease. It was his dinner-jacket. The blood throbbed, flooding over his cheeks, temples, up to the parting of his hair. He felt like an albino. There were several picture papers on the table. Weeks old. He picked one up. He had read them all. They knew that he knew that they knew he had read them all. Great God. He got up suddenly and disappeared into the smoking-room.

It was small, cold, with huge rusty spring-chairs. Time-tables. The Visitor's Book. A chart of the Islands. At worst, Victor would find there the Australian who advised them all to emigrate. But it was only Philip.

'Oh, hullo, Lindsay. You here? Good work.' Victor grinned. 'I suppose you were hiding. You know I've got a bone to pick with you.'

'You mean,' (Allen maintained that Philip always smiled at Page 'indulgently'), 'about our not turning up this afternoon?'

'I looked all round the place for you before we started.'

'Did you really? I say, I'm most awfully sorry.

30

I looked for you, too. We must have followed each other round and round.'

Victor laughed, flopping into a chair.

'Like Boy Scouts on the trail. Have a gasper? I suppose you smoke nothing but the best Turkish.'

'Why should I only smoke Turkish?' asked Philip, obscurely pleased.

'I don't know.' Victor with amiable fatuity gave it up. 'You're a luxurious sort of devil, aren't you?'

'Me? You must have funny ideas of luxury.'

Allen was incomprehensible. How could he seriously pretend to 'loathe' Page – large, grinning, harmless, one leg hooked over the chair-arm? 'But of course Allen only thinks of him as a little working model of his uncle. The worst of seeing things from one angle. I'm glad I did say that.' A kind of perverse conscientiousness made Philip add:

'But I haven't told you yet why we didn't come. At the last moment, Chalmers wasn't up to it. He's got a rotten headache.'

'Oh, hard luck.' Perhaps lest this should seem too formal, Victor asked, without curiosity: 'I suppose he turned in early to-night.'

'I expect so. I really haven't the least idea.' Philip could not resist an uneasy glance towards the window. 'Yes, I believe he did say something about it.'

The street outside was now quite dark. Some yards down, at a spot invisible from the smoking-room, a stain of light, cast through frosted glass, fell upon the opposite wall. From within proceeded gruff voices of sailors and fishermen. This was the public bar of the hotel.

'It's a pity. I don't know when you'll get another chance. The wind's changed again.'

'Oh, well. I expect we shall be staying for some time yet.'

Victor smiled and flushed slightly, as he always did when about to put a personal question.

'I suppose you're awfully keen on this place?'

'Yes. It's all right.' Philip was puzzled, not sure how to take this.

'I mean to say – I sometimes wonder what you find to do here. I never see you up at the links. And lately you've seemed rather off going excursions. Of course, I know you paint – '

'That takes up a good bit of the time.'

'Oh, of course, it must. But I mean, in the evenings and so forth.'

'Well, I write.'

('I should like to make a gramophone record of your professional modesty voice' – Allen, again.)

'I say, Lindsay, do you really? As well? Were you writing something when I came in just now?'

'Only touching up an old poem.'

Victor laughed, quite awed.

'You seem to be a regular all-round man.'

'But it really is too absurd of Allen to say that I like Page because he flatters me,' Philip thought. 'Imagine feeling flattered at his ridiculous sporting terms. One might think, to hear him talk, that one was useful in the slips.'

Into the boot-room they crowded, clumsy as puppies, wet-haired, muddy in their shorts and sweaters. Kicking sparks from the stone floor with their boot-studs. Jostling to wash their knees at the tap. What was it like on Lower? Oh, we had a juicy victory, didn't we, Flea? I scored all six. You liar. Well, Lindsay booted one of them in by mistake. Lindsay. Where's Linseed? Where's the Linseed Poultice? Pig says you booted one into your own goal. Did you? Did you? Oh, good effort. Jolly smart. Highly cute. Don't you think you were cute? Look, he's blubbing. Linseed's blubbing. The Poultice is damp. Does didums want nanna? Never mind. Hard luck, Lindsay. Cheer up Lin-

33

seed. Anyway Linseed threw in jolly well this afternoon. Yes, he did. He threw in right over Flea's head. Good old Linseed. Three cheers for Poultice. Thumping his back they clustered round a moment, grotesquely soothed him. Look out. Here's Major Frith. You're all right, aren't you, Poultice? May I ask how much longer you Juniors propose to hang round the lavatories? Out before I count ten. We're coming, sir. Sorry sir. Oh, *sir*. All clattered away.

'You know, I've often wished I could do something in that line myself.'

If Allen could have heard him!

'Have you ever tried?'

'Oh, I say,' Victor grinned but blushed, 'can you see me at it?'

'So he really has.' Philip was more than ever benignant. 'I should think at about fourteen. Walking tour in the Snowdon district. When I survey thee, awful peak. Wordsworth with Tennysonian hyphens. Or later, possibly, at school. Brooke. No, Page wouldn't be erotic.'

There was something of a pause.

'I'd like you to see my uncle's place in Surrey. It's rather decent. We've got some woods and a lake. You live in London, don't you? You ought

34

to come down some time. You might get an idea for a picture, you know.'

'I'd love to. And you must come and see us, if you're ever in town.'

'Thanks awfully. We come up in the car sometimes. And I often stay there a few days before Term begins. And then my uncle's always liable to shut up the house and leave England for a bit. He says he feels cooped up here.'

'We live in North Kensington. Bellingham Gardens. I'll write it down for you.'

Philip's home had seldom seemed less real to him than as he scribbled its address on a half-sheet of paper and handed it to Victor. 'But I suppose I shall be back there before the month's out,' he thought.

'Oh, thanks. Now you must have mine.'

After this rather clumsy little formality, Victor went on:

'I'm afraid living in Town wouldn't suit me an atom. You know, if I don't have heaps of fresh air and exercise, I get most frightfully morbid.'

'I can hardly imagine that,' Philip grinned ('indulgently?')

'Oh, but I do,' Victor nodded, seriously, smiling. 'I turn into a regular pessimist. You should see me. For that matter, I don't suppose

you care much for it either, do you? I mean you
don't get much chance of painting or writing.'

This was almost distinguished. A refinement
of naïveté. Did the man believe that you couldn't
paint indoors? Or that it was 'never done.' A
sort of Yankee trick? But Victor added:

'You haven't the time, of course.'

Could Allen – ? That was fantastic. And Page
was so plainly innocent of deeper hintings. Nevertheless, with a slightly guilty suddenness, Philip
had asked:

'How did you know about my job?'

'I didn't. Only I – well, I supposed you had
one, somehow. It never struck me. It isn't a
ghastly secret, is it?'

His face was crimson. Thinking that now he'd
put his foot in properly. One discussed such subjects always at one's own risk. If the other person suddenly turned touchy, you had no excuse.
Poor Page. Philip hastened to say:

'Of course not. I'm in an insurance office in the
city. I've been there four years now. Since I
passed the matric, with a coach. I never went to a
public school because I had rheumatic fever
twice; the first time while I was at my prepper.
It's supposed to be a very good job. People tell
me I'm lucky to have it.'

One day, young man, you'll be glad that your elders brutally chained you to the office stool. Ha, ha. 'Shall I tell Page everything? Interesting to see how he'd take it. By Jove, I've a good mind to.'

'I envy you, you know. Having anything definite, like that. Sometimes, at Cambridge, one feels rather a rotter, hanging about. Of course, it's all in a good cause, so to speak. There's the degree. But it takes such years.'

('I couldn't, though. He'd be too shocked.')

'You'd honestly be surprised at the life some men lead up there. Not only do they never condescend to do a stroke, but they lounge about all day as if the place was a sort of hôtel de luxe. It'd bore me stiff, I know that. However they appear to think they're being fearfully clever. And then some of these super-aesthetes. You know, what I think's the matter with them is that they're all fellows who've been absolute duds at their public schools, no earthly at games or anything, and now they've determined to make a bit of a splash.' Victor paused, appealing for Philip's agreement, charmingly unconscious that he was within miles of the personal. 'They wear the most ghastly clothes you ever saw and to hear them chattering in the college court you'd think there were a lot of women about the place. We've only got half-a-dozen of them in ours, thank goodness, but they fairly buy the staircase next to mine. I believe something's going to be done about it next term. It's no joke when you're in training and want to get to sleep early. The Captain of our Boat says he'll deal drastically with them if they don't make themselves jolly scarce. He's a damn sound man. You ought to have heard my uncle on the subject when he was up for the week-end. He said that if – '

Crash.

No, it was only afterwards, a second or so later, that the door seemed to have made such a noise. Really it had just knocked the edge of the small table sharply against the wall. But Philip started violently enough. Had he, subconsciously, been expecting this – for the last half-hour?

Allen was no paler than usual. He stood in the wide open doorway, calm; one hand resting on the jamb. He had been out of doors without a hat, the night breeze had ruffled his hair. One received the impression that he was about to make an announcement.

Victor said:

'Hullo, Chalmers.'

38

Allen did not seem to hear this; but he smiled faintly.

'I thought you were upstairs,' began Philip, in a false, nervous voice. It dried up into a hoarse noise in his throat. He could not go on.

Allen was silent for several moments. Then he closed his eyes. With startling violence he ejaculated the word: 'No!'

He turned his head carefully backwards and forwards, as though his neck were stiff.

'If you want to know where I've been,' he said suddenly, rather loud, 'you'd better ask my friend Lindsay about the *genuine* forms.'

He paused, then added:

'It's a very, very brilliant fallacy. They're not. The view-points are epicentric. Professor Whitehead. I absolutely but unconditionally agree.'

Philip had risen and Victor was beside him.

'I suppose this is Greek to you, Page. Far too long to explain here. We were discussing a rock. Immensely intricate. One ordinary boatman.' Rather surprisingly, Allen's elbow relaxed. He stumbled against the door-post, then perfectly recovered. 'Take his other arm,' said Victor, huskily.

There were three people in the lounge. All women. Their figures, seated, bent forward, deeply engrossed in needlework, as the young men came out of the smoking-room. The place appeared to have shrunk slightly smaller, and to be unnaturally quiet. It was as if Philip himself were a little intoxicated. He could imagine the women's eyes following them. They steered Allen to the foot of the stairs. Feeling their support, he lolled, sliding his feet. Victor had gone pale, this time. They avoided each other's glance.

'Oh, I know you think this is a gesture,' Allen shouted, when they were half-way up. He was troublesome and kept trying to kneel on the steps. Victor patiently hauled him to his feet. Later, he remarked, in a more reasonable voice:

'The thing one had to get quite clear is that the interest was exclusively psychological.'

They were in his room, now. Philip switched on the light. Allen sat heavily upon the bed. He seemed prepared to go to sleep.

'Will he be all right?' asked Victor, in an undertone.

Philip did not feel certain, but he said, at once: 'Yes, perfectly, thanks' – wishing to reassure Page, who was obviously wondering whether he ought to offer to help Chalmers undress.

Outside the door, for the first time, they looked each other in the face. Philip had a momentary rather hysterical desire to grin. But Victor's expression quelled it. Page was not shocked. He was disgusted.

'Good-night,' he said, briefly, turning on his heel. He strode down the passage with large steps, as if he wanted to get away, as quickly as possible, from both of them.

CHAPTER III

A ND there you sit,' cried Philip.

He walked with impatience to the bedroom window. Out across the pool, overswept with blurred, refracted beams, the steamer lay within the pier's crooked finger. Samson and Bryher showed faintly blue, remote as the volcano peaks that rise beyond the shore of a lake in Mexico. The morning scene was delicately pencilled, luminous, insipid, resembling a watercolour by an elderly gentlewoman.

'Sorry. I didn't know it was annoying you.'

Allen, who had been lolling on the bed in his shirt-sleeves, holding the shaving-brush between finger and thumb, rose lazily and began to lather his chin. After a minute, he said:

'I had nothing but beer and whiskey and a little gin. It's only sherry which upsets me. Besides, you know, apart from poetic justice, you wouldn't really have liked it if I'd been sick. Not at the time.'

'I'm sure I shouldn't have cared two damns if you'd had d.t.'s on the spot.'

Allen paused and screwed together his safety-razor. Philip turned from the window.

'I simply fail to conceive what made you do it.

Was it for a joke, or to be clever, or merely out of spite?'

Allen considered:

'Why does one? I don't know. Something sets you going on the first three glasses, and the rest's more or less automatic. Boredom, usually. Then there's a certain atmosphere about it. Baudelaire. Poor Edgar, my namesake. Very childish. You don't approve of all that, of course. It's debased romanticism.'

'I suppose you'll think me unreasonable to remind you of the fact; but you did incidentally promise at dinner that if you went on drinking you'd go straight from the public bar up to bed.'

'Yes, I remember that. But I believe I wanted to tell you something. About our artistic discussion yesterday afternoon. Ideas occurred to me.'

'They did, evidently.'

'Why? Tell me,' Allen grinned through soap, 'did I say anything really amusing? In front of Page?'

Philip broke out again, frowning:

'Yes. To you, quite naturally, this is just — amusing.'

'Certainly it isn't. Not altogether. But what am I to do? I've said I'm sorry four times. And

43

I am, really, Philip. I'll say it again, if you like.
I'm perfectly sincere.'

'As if that did any good.'

'No, I know it doesn't. Only now that everything's over, there hardly seems much else one
can – '

'Everything over?' Philip drily laughed. 'You
don't look very far ahead.'

'Where am I to look?'

'Well, what do you propose to do when you
leave this room?'

'Have breakfast, of course.'

'In the dining-room?'

'No. Under the bath.'

'Don't be an idiot.'

'Well, you really ask such extraordinary ques-
ons. Where did you suppose I should have
it?'

'Oh, I understand,' Philip was worked up, now.
'You're still drunk.'

'I am, very slightly. But not enough to affect
this discussion. My brain's perfectly clear.'

Philip walked back to the window. He would
not answer.

'I'm sorry I was flippant. I understood you
perfectly. You mean that the Pages will be there.
But, honestly, I shan't object to meeting them, in

44

the least. I'm afraid you over-rate me. I've got no delicacy of that sort.'

'I meant that it's a question whether Page'll have the decency to stay in the same room with you.'

'He'll be very uncomfortable if he doesn't. The lounge tables are frightfully small.'

Philip, in this theatrical mood, was too comic to annoy. Nevertheless, his idea was offensive. Allen paused in his shaving and added, with some emphasis:

'I should be glad to know what business it is of Page's anyway.'

'If he hadn't made it his business last night, you'd have slept in the street.'

'Nonsense. I only lolled and made myself extra heavy because I wanted to annoy him. I remember that quite clearly. I should have got upstairs much better with you alone. You ought to be tight once or twice, Philip. The psychology of drunkenness is really amazing.'

'Do you know,' said Philip, coldly, 'that there were several ladies in the lounge while you were kicking up all that fuss?'

'Do them good. If I'd noticed, I'd have pretended to try and rape one. Was that girl there who sings Schubert? Seriously, what possible harm –

Page is turning you into a regular little gentleman.'

'I must say you rather overdo the professional cad touch.'

Allen finished shaving with rapid strokes, sponged his face and put on a collar.

'Page's decency must get some steep tests at Cambridge, when drunks invade his rooms at 3 a.m. and start putting the furniture up the chimney.'

'There's some slight difference between Cambridge and a hotel where women are staying.'

'You mimic his voice wonderfully,' said Allen, with admiration.

Philip turned his back, too angry to retort. Far off, across the harbour, a deep hollow moan reverberated, ceased.

'One hour,' Allen leisurely drew on his pullover. 'Have you packed?'

'I suppose you flatter yourself that I shall change my mind at the last minute.'

'I certainly hope you won't. My suitcase is heavy. I don't want to have to drag it down to the pier for nothing.'

'Oh, so you are coming?'

'Unless you'd rather I didn't.'

'I don't in the least care either way. But I'm a

little surprised that you're leaving the hotel –
since you're so indifferent to what everybody
thinks of you.'

'If I'd been by myself I'd have left it the day
after the Pages came.'

Allen was now quite ready.

'Come along down,' he said, 'we'll have breakfast first and pack afterwards. There's plenty of
time.'

'My good man, you don't seriously suppose
I've the face to go into that dining-room again.
Everybody in the house must know.'

'Just as you like. I'll have something sent up
here for you.'

'And have that chambermaid in? She'll know.
Not likely. I don't intend to speak to another
soul in the place. I imagine you won't object to
fixing up our bills. If you haven't enough cash,
you'll find some in the leather wallet on my
dressing-table.'

'But, Philip, you must eat something. You
can't do a three hours' steamer trip on an empty
stomach. It's sure to be fairly rough. Don't be
pig-headed.'

'I can't help that.'

'Look here. I'll bring up something myself.
I'll tell them you don't want to be disturbed.'

47

'For Heaven's sake don't make us any more conspicuous than we are already. Personally, I've no intention of eating a mouthful until we've left this island.'

'Oh, all right, then.'

Allen put his hands into his pockets and went downstairs.

'Philip, Blessed Saint and Martyr,' he thought. On waking, that morning, Allen had made up his mind to bear a good deal. He was, even more than usual, completely in the wrong. But after an hour and a half of this kind of conversation, his patience was slightly raw. Philip had come in barely ten minutes after he had opened his eyes.

'Good morning, sir.'

The waiter, a very nice man, who had been in a large London hotel and had taken this post for his health, grinned discreetly, but with a distinct gleam of approval. Philip was right.

When Allen was half-way through breakfast, Victor came in and sat down at his far-off table. They were alone together in the dining-room, for it was still early. He kept his eyes intently on his plate.

Allen's pulse quickened slightly, though not with shame. He was thinking that it would be amusing to speak to Page on the way out. What should he say? 'Ten thousand thanks for seeing me through, old boy, last night. I was . . . a bit of a beast, I'm afraid . . . I . . .' Bad taste is a minor social art; to be practised for its own sake. 'But I suppose I mustn't,' Allen decided regretfully. 'After all, he's Philip's property now. I've even forfeited the right to insult him.'

And so, while Victor stared at the cruet-stand, cursing his complexion, Allen walked leisurely up the room in silence, comfortably aware of having eaten porridge, two helpings of eggs and kidneys, marmalade and toast.

Another distant moan of the steamer's siren. Half an hour had passed.

Philip had finished his packing and was nervously prowling about in Allen's bedroom, smoking cigarettes.

'You've been an incredibly long time,' he said, peevishly.

Allen began to fill his suitcase in an abstracted manner and with a misapplied ingenuity, putting the tube of toothpaste into a bedroom slipper and carefully rolling his pyjamas into a lump of unnatural bulk. Philip fidgeted.

'For Heaven's sake be quick.'

'What shall we do,' asked Allen, 'if the Pages, out of respect for our feelings, have decided to leave by this morning's boat?'

When he was ready, they had less than twenty minutes to spare. Allen led the way along the passage. It was empty. Down the staircase. The waiter was in the hall. Already tipped, he smiled: 'Good-bye, gentlemen. Pleasant voyage.' Out into the deserted street.

'Oh, God,' exclaimed Philip, when they were nearly half-way down to the quay : 'My easel.'

He had always kept it downstairs, resting along two coat-hooks, in a small passage leading from the lounge to the terrace door. Panting, he crossed the hall. It was there.

Victor, from a corner of the lounge, sitting alone, saw him enter. Heavens; he felt awkward. But an impulse that was slightly guilty made him rise to his feet and advance:

'You off, Lindsay? Cheer-ho. Hope you have a decent crossing.'

Ought one to say anything else? If so, what on earth – ? He had an inspiration:

'I say, I shall make a point of looking you up you know, when next we're in town.'

That was it. To make Lindsay feel he didn't, in the least, because of last night. Just right for once. Victor mentally patted himself on the back. And Lindsay seemed pleased:

'Oh, do. That'll be awfully nice. Good-bye till then.'

He was really a very decent little man. And, under the circumstances, jolly sporting to stick to Chalmers.

Down the cobbled street they hurried again, and out into the wind, along the broad-flagged pier, stacked with barrels, crates, baskets and great coils of tarred cable. The gangway was dragged up less than a minute after they had crossed it.

In silence they stood at the rail while the steamer backed slowly, through churned foam. The pier-head crowd receded; idlers and waving girls. Strangers. A purely sexual farewell. 'No,' thought Allen, 'one could never, under any circumstances, regret leaving any place.' Northward, rounding Crow Rock; between the wooded and the barren shore.

'I say, where are we going?'

'I should have thought that was rather obvious.'

'Not to me, I'm afraid.'

'That is,' Philip corrected himself, 'I know where *I'm* going. London.'

'You don't mean at once?'

'Certainly, I do. If this boat runs to time, I ought to get a train arriving in town about eleven-thirty to-night.'

'But, Philip, it's absurd. You'll be dog-tired for no reason. And everyone'll be in bed by the time you get to the house.'

'So much the better. I shan't see them till the morning.'

'And what will your mother say?'

'I really neither know nor care.'

'You do know, and you'll probably be made to care considerably. You agreed yesterday afternoon that she'd take at any rate another fortnight to, well – see things from your point of view.'

'Yesterday afternoon the whole situation was entirely different.'

'Oh, granted this is all my doing. But, look here, Philip, it really is preposterous. You're *making* things unpleasant for yourself. Why on earth need you go home yet? There's dozens of places nearby on the mainland where we could spend another week or two, at least. And you'd find the same sort of things to paint. If I cramp your style, I'll go on by myself to town. But for goodness' sake don't mess up all your plans because of this business. It's so idiotic. It's really childish.'

But Philip had made up his mind. His profile was as obstinate as Allen had ever seen it. He said in his most snobbish, 'stuffy' voice:

'You don't in the least understand.'

It was no use talking to him in this condition. Allen answered:

'As you say, I most certainly don't,' and strolled away along the deck.

.   .   .   .

An hour later, they were well on their course. The little steamer was dipping and rolling through a heavy swell, plunging ahead with sickening oscillations. There were not now so many of the passengers to be seen. Allen stood by himself, smoking his pipe, as he watched the last of the humped-backed islands disappear, veiled in rain.

Poor Philip was somewhere below, retching miserably from his empty stomach. He had worn his martyr's crown for several days. Now he was earning it.

CHAPTER IV

WHEN the train arrived, Joan at once noticed that her brother looked fatter, and was glad, at any rate, that the change had done him good.

'You wouldn't have said so if you'd seen him yesterday. It's the effect of a night at the Imperial Grand Parade Hotel.'

Crowds jostled them. Their faces were smiling, dazed.

'You need a new hat,' she told Allen.

'Do I?' He took it off and seemed surprised by its stains. 'Can you buy them near here?'

'I don't know.' Joan shook her head, grinning dumbly. They were all three drifting down the platform. The meeting had been blurred, as in a dream. But before they got into a cab, Philip's easel slid between someone's legs, tripping them, and Allen found time to say :

'I suppose you're all furious with me?'

'Are we? You haven't been discussed much. I expect Mother isn't very pleased.'

Holding the door open, he asked:

'And are you?'

'Oh, you're not important enough,' she answered, smiling quickly, 'to be worth my consideration. All the same,' this was out of the window, 'I think, if you don't mind, you'd better not come to the house for a week or two, at any rate. You quite understand, don't you?'

'Oh, quite,' he smiled and waved his hand, rather ironically.

They drove off and Allen turned, smoking his pipe, in the direction of the Underground Railway. A thin figure with curiously broad shoulders, he was soon lost amongst the crowd.

Inside the cab, Philip was asking:

'How on earth did you know we should arrive to-day?'

'Allen sent me a note this morning. Why' — Joan seemed amused — 'didn't you want me to come and meet you, Phil?'

'Oh, of course. That is, I'm glad you have. As a matter of fact, our plans kept changing practically every few hours. I wasn't in the least sure that I'd come up to-day, even late last night. Allen seems to have taken it on himself to prophesy.'

Picking a scrap of fluff from his coat collar, she said :

'You left sooner than you'd meant, didn't you?'

'Yes.'

She noticed the faint curtness of his tone, and

55

that he had shaved his little side-whiskers. There was a considerable pause.

At length Philip spoke as casually as possible, looking out of the cab window:

'Mother got my note, of course.'

'Oh, yes,' Joan couldn't help smiling, 'in fact, a bit too quickly. You gave it me at the corner, you remember, when I was seeing you into the taxi. Well, like an idiot, I brought it straight back and handed it to her on the spot.'

'But, Joan, I especially said keep it till the evening.'

'I know you did. But I didn't take that in properly at the time. I'd thought I should forget and carry it about in my pocket for days. And I could have kicked myself when it was opened. But there you are. Somehow it never crossed my head that it was anything really important.'

'I suppose you mean that I ought to have told you?'

'Ought you? I don't see why. It wasn't anything to do with me.'

'But you understand why I didn't? It wouldn't have been fair to you, would it? I mean, that if you'd known, you'd have felt you ought to tell Mother beforehand.'

His tone had been quite rude; as always, when

he was rather ashamed of himself. Now it was anxious, conciliatory. He was anxious that she should accept his probably semi-insincere explanations. Joan was scarcely conscious of how well she knew how to manage her brother. She had grown up in the art. I hope you realize I've bagged first on the bike this morning. I suppose you think *you* ought to have it because you're the eldest? Of course I don't, stupid. Boys always come before girls. Rot, you don't believe that. Yes I do. Girls can't do things like boys. Boys always get their own way. Oh, well, when boys are gentlemen, like me, they give way to girls. Besides I was only ragging. You can have first if you want it, you know.

She agreed readily:

'Yes, you're quite right, Phil, I should.'

But her own feelings did not interest her. She was concerned about Philip. Although so clever, perhaps even a genius (she did not pretend to judge) he was certainly very unpractical. He did not seem to have the smallest conception of the row he had caused at home. It would surprise him.

'So you do understand,' he persisted.

'Oh, of course. Of course.' She good-humouredly checked this fussing. 'But, as I was saying,

Mother got your letter about twenty minutes after you'd left the house. And at first I really had great difficulty in persuading her not to take another taxi and pay the man double fare to be at Paddington before the train started. She wanted to catch you and make you come home and discuss the whole thing.'

'Good God,' Philip was frankly scared, 'did she really?'

'Yes; and so then we decided that she'd better ring up the office and make quite sure that you'd given up your job. I mean, it seemed just possible that we'd entirely misunderstood your note.'

'Heavens ! I should have thought what I wrote was plain enough for a baby.'

'Well, I daresay. Mother and I are both fairly dense. But you know, Phil, some of the expressions you used were rather general. You just said:"I've decided to chuck everything up." And when a letter's important it seems to have so many meanings.'

'I must say – '

'Well, anyhow, we got on to Mr. Eliott, and he was most awfully nice; and said how sorry they were to lose you and how they hoped you'd have every success in your new career. (We didn't tell him anything, of course.) So that settled that. There was nothing to be done but wait until you got back.'

'I see. But now that I am – I say, Joan, I hope to goodness Mother doesn't imagine that this affair isn't settled? I mean, she isn't going to try and argue about it, is she?'

'I'm afraid she may do just a little, at first.'

'Because it's no earthly good.'

'No, I told her it wouldn't be, if you'd made up your mind. But you know what Mother is, don't you, Phil?'

'I do most certainly.'

Philip was gloomily silent, playing with the upholstered handstrap at his elbow. He was glad that they had a cab, not a taxi. It was becoming increasingly clear to him that he did not want this drive to end.

'Does Langbridge know?' he asked presently.

'No. Mother hasn't told him.'

'Why the devil not?' His nervous uneasiness showed clearly in this petulance. 'She doesn't suppose she can hush this up from him, does she? I never heard anything so idiotic. Why, by this time, he'll have dropped in to see Eliott and found out for himself.'

'Well, as it happens, he's been out of town this

last fortnight. He'll be back in another week. But you see, Mother put off writing to him, just on the chance.'

'The chance of what?'

'That you'd come home.'

'But I don't in the least understand. What earthly difference does my coming home make?'

'Well, you see, Phil, she's waiting to see whether you really mean to give up business.'

'My God, this is intolerable! I must say, Joan, I do think you might have managed to impress that much on her. You know how I loathe these scenes.'

'I'm sorry. I tried.'

'Of course. I know she's as obstinate as a pig.'

Joan allowed the violence of this outburst to dissipate a little before she asked:

'By the way, Phil, what *are* you going to do exactly? It's ridiculous of me not to know.'

'I'm going to write and paint.'

'Oh, yes – '

She had been prepared for something more definite, but her tone was acquiescent. She had said already that it was not her business. Philip, on his side, wished that she had not accepted it so quietly. In his present mood, it would have done him good to be contradicted or, at least, questioned. He felt the need of making a declaration.

'Of course, I've planned everything out very carefully. I'm prepared to run this on strictly commercial lines. It's got to pay. It will pay, sooner or later. I shall place articles and stories with magazines and I shall sell my pictures. It's only a question of time and of influence. One wants to know a few people. All I ask is that Mother shall keep me for six months. By then I guarantee at least to be earning my board. Mind you, this is purely an experiment. If I'm no good I shan't go on fooling about.'

Joan nodded, impressed. She could kindle easily to his moods, and this speech had done them both good, like a sip of brandy. She was eager to encourage him.

'And I'm sure Mother would let you have the box-room for a studio, now that you're going to be at home all day. It faces north, doesn't it? And there's the skylight as well.'

Philip frowned dubiously.

'I'd rather hoped to get a room out somewhere. One can't work in the house. If Mother isn't coming in and out with a duster to see whether the maids have been along the mantelpiece,

there's Currants wanting to know a word of three
letters meaning wicked.'

'Yes, of course. But I don't quite know if that
could be managed. You see, it would mean a lot
of extra expense. And as it is – well, I mean,
while you had your job you were getting – '

'You mean I'm behaving badly about the cash?'

'Phil, I never said – '

'Well, before you start, please do me the justice
to think for a few minutes. People a lot worse off
than we are send their sons to the Varsity and
keep them there for three or four years. When
have I been kept? Why, even at a public school
I should have cost more than I did with a tutor.
It really is a bit too thick – '

He broke off and began again:

'I admit this is a defeat. I've tried the City.
I'm no good at it. Very well. But why spend
the whole of the rest of my life crying over spilt
milk? I have simply to try something else,
something that I am some good at, or believe I
am. Otherwise, nothing has any meaning. After
all, it's sheer optimism to suppose that one's
going to find what kind of work one wants to do
at the first shot – '

Philip stopped abruptly. The thought that
they were only in a cab; that he had not yet met

his mother; that all this talk was a mere rehearsal of arguments which must be used again and against opposition; that, in short, the whole question, which yesterday seemed over and settled, had not yet been faced, checked him like an iron key slipped down his back, inside the vest.

They were nearing home now. The cab trundled through gay slum streets, shrill with the febrile games of sickly children. At the corner of the main thoroughfare the old stucco-faced brothel presented to the sunlight its faded respectability of maidenhair fern-pots and discoloured Venetian blinds.

'Cheer up, Phil. I don't believe Mother really minds half as much as she makes out.'

Philip replied crossly:

'I don't care how much she minds.'

Nevertheless, he received a certain base comfort from her words.

The cab turned into Bellingham Gardens.

It was a long downhill slope, bordered along either pavement with lopped plane trees. Looking from the high ground one's eye travelled into uncertain distance, beyond low-lying fields and tennis-courts set apart for the employees of a large West End stores. A gas-works rose sombrely amidst pavilions and changing-sheds. Allen had once named it The Boulevard.

'I do hope someone'll have got some tea ready,' said Joan.

They had arrived. She paid the cabman and led the way into the house.

'Now,' thought Philip, as he followed her.

But they met no one. In the sitting-room, tea was laid for three, and one cup had been used.

'Mother's about somewhere. I suppose I'd better go and look for her.'

'Oh, no, Phil. Have something to eat first.'

He dropped into a chair and took the cup and plate which she handed him. The thought: 'a rearguard action,' made him smile. His spirits rose a little. He glanced round the familiar room, appraising its humorous possibilities. There were a crowd of armchairs and two sofas, all covered in bright cretonne, with frills – suggesting the pretty, fresh, summer dresses of pre-war girls. The water-colour drawings – Sussex and Venice – had gilt mounts. Silver-framed photographs stood on the mantelpiece and on several little mahogany tables, together with silver and ivory paper-knives, stork-scissors, shagreen leather work boxes with silver monogram, mother-of-pearl ashtrays. Inlaid bureau and book-case, containing a leather-bound, gold-patterned, India paper uniform edition of Shakespeare, Boswell, Montaigne, Bacon's *Essays*, the Divine Comedy, Elia, the Plague Year, *Tristram Shandy* and Keats' Letters – at least thirty volumes. A lamp in the form of a Corinthian column, silver, with a pleated rose silk shade. Mrs. Lindsay disliked reading by electric light. On the Broadwood cottage upright a Breton ware bowl of tulips.

Philip suddenly rose, crossed to it and struck half-a-dozen minor chords.

'That'll let everybody know I'm back.'

But the piano wanted tuning and its sound, echoing in the still, closed room, was hollow as his impulse of bravado. A moment, and both died away.

'Aren't you going to eat any more?' asked Joan in some concern.

'No. I think I'll get my unpacking done.'

Philip climbed wearily the thirty steps to his bedroom. On the landing he came face to face with his mother. She had been waiting for him there. The meeting had no drama, for both had passed the climax of anticipation. For some moments neither spoke. Then Philip said:

'Hullo.' They regarded each other blankly.

Mrs. Lindsay, once pretty, was now small,

pale, grey-haired. She powdered her nose without skill, leaving visible grains and streaks of rawness. The lines of her face suggested pathos, boredom and nervous irritability. She screwed them now into an expression intended to be scornful, actually merely ugly.

'So you've come back?'

He nodded. Suddenly, he had felt physically tired all over. It was as if they had already been talking for hours. He regarded her stupidly, intently, confused by irrelevant memories, associations suggested by the stair-carpet, the lithographs and the little rugs. A queer atrophy of the will. There seemed nothing to say. He thought: 'I'm being hypnotized.'

Watching her son's face, she flung out emotionally:

'No wonder you were afraid to tell us what you'd done.'

Philip said nothing.

'And now' – the sound of her own plaintive voice was giving her confidence – 'what's your next scheme? What do you imagine is going to happen to you? Have you thought of that? Who do you think is going to help you next?'

Philip roused himself, with cowardice and distaste, to answer her.

'I'm going to help myself.'

Again she made the scornful grimace.

'Oh! And since when have you ever done that?'

'It's time I started.'

'It is, certainly.'

But she had over-reached herself here and had quickly to guard with:

'So what do you mean to do?'

'You know quite well. I want to have a chance of painting and writing.'

'Painting and writing!' She shied like a little pony at the words. 'How are you to live?'

'I suppose I can sell my work.'

'You've been doing a lot while you were away, of course?'

'Of course,' he lied.

Her question, as in older, earlier quarrels, had seemed telepathic. She regarded him for a moment, searchingly. But next she asked:

'Whatever made you do it?'

'Because I loathed the office. I told you so over and over again.'

This is how talk ends, carefully made plans, arguments discussed night after night. I do want to make Mother admit that I'm right; and really it's difficult to see how any reasonable adult could conceivably. There *can* be nothing for her to say. Now here he was, answering like a half-scared insolent schoolboy.

'Is that all?'

'Yes, of course.'

'Are you quite sure?'

'Of course I'm sure.' He was puzzled.

'There isn't – anything else, is there? I'm your mother, Philip. I think I've a right to know.'

Her voice, though harsh, had a certain eagerness. Would she have preferred that to this? The definite to the indefinite? At least, then, the situation would have been plainer. The suggestion, in Philip's present mood, could not even make him smile. Nevertheless, she saw, at once, her mistake. Already, perplexed and overwrought, she had been near to tears. She easily shed them now.

'You don't know how you've hurt me.'

He stood before her; bored, shamed, wishing only to get away. Presently, she recovered herself a little:

'How are you going to explain all this to people?'

'To Mr. Langbridge? You haven't told him?'

'Naturally not; what could I say to him?'

'Nothing.'

'And I don't know what you'll say, I'm sure.'

'Neither do I.'

She flared up at this, dispirited though his tone had been.

'Oh, you're impossible!'

She turned and went downstairs with a small gesture of irritation that seemed a mere comma in their argument; inconclusive, leaving nearly everything still to be said.

CHAPTER V

PALE amongst Edwardian cretonnes, Mrs.
Lindsay sat at the inlaid bureau, her husband's wedding present, reckoning domestic
accounts with inflamed eyes, by a failing light.

Mary Durrant was in the bath. She had had
one yesterday, and it was a waste of hot water,
but where else was she to go? It was raining. The
weather had turned chilly. Dorothy did not like
her to use the gas-fire in her bedroom before
dinner. And Dorothy hadn't seemed to want
her company in the sitting-room. She hadn't
even a book to read. Philip had been going to
lend her one, but she didn't like to go down
and ask him for it, because Dorothy had been
heard saying very distinctly to the servants that
morning:

'Mr. Philip wants to be left *absolutely* alone in
future. His room isn't to be touched, unless he
gives you orders himself.'

So she sighed and washed her hair; wishing,
in the middle of the tiresome process, that she
had not begun, and deciding, quite finally, to
have it bobbed.

'Wonder what's up?' said the maid to the cook,
over strong, late tea. 'I do 'ope there 'asn't been
a death in the famerly.'

'Death? Wait till you've been 'ere six months, my girl. Death, indeed. You won't catch 'em.'

In Philip's sitting-room the atmosphere was bluish and stale. He had smoked cigarettes until his head ached; gone on smoking until he felt merely stupid. On an easel by the window stood the harbour picture (which, after all, Allen had liked.) And on the table, littered with books and papers, were three and a half pages of Philip's manuscript. The whole place was in a mess. The door locked. He had been reading a novel for the last four hours.

Just before dinner, Joan came in from her classes at the School of Cookery.

'You look awfully tired, Phil,' she said, meeting her brother on the stairs.

The remark frightened him. He was easily worried about his health. If this were to go on for long, he wouldn't be able to stand it. Suppose he had a nervous breakdown? This would, of course, impress them; but, at the same time, it might be serious. How does one get brain fever? Allen would know.

But he was not ready to see Allen again yet.

Dinner. Slices of fatty cold beef. Boiled rice, with jam. It could hardly be unintentional. Especially as the jam was gooseberry. Philip

71

refused both, eating cheese and biscuits. Mrs. Lindsay seemed not to notice. Joan thought it best to say nothing. Miss Durrant remarked: 'I'm afraid the sea air's taken away all Phil's appetite.'

She beamed anxiously, tomato-cheeked behind rimless pince-nez, and looked round for agreement to their lowered faces:

'Or is it that you've been working too hard? What have you been so busy at the last two days? Is it a great secret? When are we to know?'

Philip glanced up and said with a straying eye on his mother:

'I'm writing a novel.'

'How *thrilling!* What about? Or mustn't we hear that?'

'Well' – Philip smiled agreeably – he could always be agreeable to Currants. 'Perhaps the subject's hardly suitable for your ears. Put baldly.'

'But aren't we *ever* going to hear it, then?'

She never knew when to take him seriously. The darling boy was so brilliantly clever; he often talked above one's head without knowing it.

'Oh, of course. When the book's finished. My line of treatment will be reticent.'

She could not make much of this either; so asked:

'And when *will* it be finished?'

'In about eighteen months.'

Philip was bland. A little discouraged, she hastened on with:

'I call that splendid. I'm sure it will be a great success. And when it's published we shall be awfully proud of him, shan't we, Dorothy?'

Mrs. Lindsay said nothing. Her lips were trembling. This was more than she could bear.

Aware, at last, that the situation had its depths, Miss Durrant plunged for the safe ground of domestic pathos:

'Mumsie's tired,' she murmured to Philip and Joan.

Nevertheless, another day was over. Philip went downstairs in heavy thought. He would have liked to talk to Joan, but she did not know it, and left him to himself. Later, he would slip out and buy some chocolate, for he was hungry. 'This is, quite technically speaking, a blockade.' The manuscript, covered mostly with erasures, lay where he had left it. The fire had gone out, demonstrating the maid's obedience to instructions. He had the impulse to cheer himself with a dance record on the gramophone. But Mrs.

73

Lindsay would hear it and know that he was not at work. This reminded Philip that he had forgotten to lock the door. He did so as noisily as possible, for the benefit of the kitchen. Lighting a fresh cigarette, he seated himself at the table and tried to summon up a little interest in the pages before him. 'Eighteen months,' he thought. 'At this rate it'll take three years.'

But, meanwhile – the appalling idea occurred to him that his mother might have the strength of purpose, or call it obstinacy, to prolong this state of affairs, if necessary, for an indefinite period. She might simply do nothing. But no. 'After all,' Philip consoled himself, 'she must be a good deal impressed already by the line I've taken.'

The question was: How much impressing would she need? A week? A fortnight? 'I couldn't keep this up for more than a month, at the outside.'

On the morning of the third day, it was raining harder than ever. At breakfast, Philip had tried addressing his mother directly. She would answer if spoken to. He asked her if she thought it would rain for long. She replied: 'I don't know.' Her tone was neither reproachful nor hostile.

She spoke as though someone in the next room were dying.

He went downstairs. The basement light in such weather was scarcely good enough to paint by. Besides, he did not want to paint. He looked long and thoughtfully at his manuscript. Then he tore it up into tiny pieces and flung them into the air, creating an artificial snowstorm. Childishly, the effect raised his spirits. He unlocked the door, put on his hat and coat, and hurried out of the house. He was recklessly aware, as he opened the gate, of Mrs. Lindsay's face at the sitting-room window.

The restaurant was a good one and he went afterwards to stalls at a farce, returning from it in a mood of irresponsibility which did not dissolve but merely became gloomy as he approached his home. There was not much left now of the money he had saved for his official 'ten days' holiday' from the office.

'How's the novel?' asked Currants, at dinner.

'Very well, thank you. To-day I did a whole chapter.'

But Mrs. Lindsay only looked hurt. Even pin-pricking was not amusing.

When the meal was over, Joan followed him down to his room.

'What am I to do?' he asked her.

'Oh, Phil, we must stop things going on like this, somehow.'

'Yes, but how?'

She was suddenly decisive:

'You must write to Mr. Langbridge.'

'Me? Joan, I can't.'

'But really, you must. He's a sensible man. And he's awfully clever at something in the City. You must tell him all the things you told me – about what you want to do, and why you left the business. He'll understand. I'm sure he will.'

'He won't.'

'I promise you he will. Besides, anyhow, he's got to be told. And it's better that you should explain to him what's happened than that Mother should.'

'Mother wouldn't explain.'

'Of course, she wouldn't. Besides, there's this. She believes a lot in what Mr. Langbridge says. If he agrees with you, then she'll change round too and you can be friends.'

'But he'll side with her.'

'Well, anyhow, it'll be a decision. It'll be something definite to go on.'

'That's true.'

Already, as though this were the solution of

everything, Philip was beginning to feel an immense relief. But he continued:

'Mind you, I need every bit of my time. Just because I don't want to be cooped up in this room all day, it doesn't mean I could be at a job. One must move about and see things. Get ideas. Go to theatres, cinemas. One's mind's got to be free. Oh, it's so obvious. But, of course, nobody understands. How can you, unless you paint or write yourself? People think an artist ought to sit on a stool and do his seven hours like an office clerk.'

Joan nodded; realizing that, as so often, he was addressing not her but their mother.

.   .   .   .

Philip woke next morning with a chill on the liver and a sick headache. He came down to breakfast passive and rather dazed.

After the meal, and when Joan had left for her classes, he found himself entering the sitting-room. He had no sense of any resolution taken. It was so easy. His mother was already there, by the fire.

'It's cold to-day,' he said dully.

'Yes, it is.'

'It might be January.'

'Yes.'

She did not raise her eyes from the grate as she spoke. Her tone was flat and colourless. He looked more closely and saw that two tears were running silently down her cheeks.

'What do you want me to do?' he asked, with weary patience.

She shook her head, biting her lips and weeping.

'Would you like me to write to Mr. Langbridge?'

She recovered herself at this sufficiently to say:

'Yes. I think it would be a very good thing if you would.'

'I'll tell him everything. And if he agrees with me, shall you admit that I've been right?'

'You know that I'm always ready to admit anything is right which I see has been for your good.' She sighed, and gazed once more into the fire.

'Yes,' Philip insisted, 'but shall you believe it, really?'

'I'm afraid one can't always force one's self to do that. I must try to, I suppose.'

They were silent for some moments. Then Mrs. Lindsay said:

'Your father always hoped that you would make a position for yourself in the world.'

'But, Mother, that's exactly what I'm trying to do. Leaving the office was the first step.'

'And I'd so wanted to see you safely launched.' Mrs. Lindsay smiled sadly at the metaphor, 'before . . . anything happens to me.'

'Well, I hope you will.'

Smiling, with a conscious wistfulness, she gazed into the fire's glowing castles.

'I know what it is. When one's young one wants to have all the fun out of life one possibly can. It's only natural. And it isn't till you grow older that you begin to see how true that old proverb is of the Hare and the Tortoise. The people who've idled about and wasted away their time, get left behind – After all, I suppose we've all been put here for a purpose. We weren't given our lives for nothing.'

A neuralgic twinge had begun over Philip's left eye. Feeling giddy, he sat down beside his mother on the sofa.

'I know it's often been hard for you, darling. We're not well off and I can't give you all the things I should like to. I know that you don't have a very lively time here. There aren't lots of dances and parties for you, like other young men have. . . . But, remember, it's hard for me, too. It's not that I'd grudge you anything. You don't think that, do you? I do try so hard to give you all your little comforts and pleasures. And naturally I'm upset when I find you don't like your home. . . . I'm afraid perhaps I was hasty in what I said at first – but I was upset. I know you won't remember that. We're going to forget it – both of us.'

Yes, yes. She conceded; appeared to plead. He was too unwell, this morning, to have detected the exact moment at which the issue had become hopelessly, inextricably, confused. Treacle soaking through skeins of wool. She wanted him to kiss her cheek. He did so.

'I shan't remember anything.'

His weakness moved her. She emitted a primitive, glabrous sound as they embraced.

'My darling boy.'

As soon as possible, Philip went up to his bedroom and lay down. Ten minutes later, he was vomiting. After this, he felt much better.

.   .   .   .

Later that day, he began a letter to Mr. Langbridge. Bored at first with the task, he became rather interested and even found it amusing, as

though this were a problem set in a literary competition. He made several drafts, trying to put
the case as lucidly as possible. He did not, however, show the finished work to anyone.

This, by return, was Mr. Langbridge's reply:

'MY DEAR PHILIP,

'Very many thanks for your letter, which I got
this morning.

'Of course, I am extremely glad that you have
come to me for advice, altho' I could wish
you had done so a little sooner – preferably,
before having taken this most important step.
However, "better late than never," and I shall
do my best to help you.

'I will take your points one by one.

'First, you say that you did not like being in the
office and were dissatisfied with your work there.
I, as you know, have been in the City now for
many years, and I am sure that you will believe
me when I tell you that your office premises are
well above the average in every way. They are
clean, light, cheerful and well ventilated. I do
not know much of the other members of the staff,
but they have always seemed to me to be very
decent people. As for your employer – he and I
are very old friends (we were at Harrow together!)

and I am sure that you would not find anywhere a kinder or fairer man. I am glad to see that you yourself admit this.

'I can well sympathize with your feelings about the work. When I was your age (a good long time ago, now!) I very often used to get depressed and generally "fed up" with myself. I shouldn't worry too much about these attacks of "the blues." Every young fellow who cares at all about getting on in the world is bound to have them sometimes. One is apt to get rather musty through being indoors all day. If you take my advice, you will get as much fresh air in your spare time as you possibly can. Try walking some of the way home from work. And join a cricket or tennis club this summer. There's nothing like exercise to blow the cobwebs away!

'Secondly, you say that it was necessary for you to act as you did because nothing would have been settled while you were still at the office, and that it would have been impossible to get your mother's consent to your leaving it. I am afraid I cannot altogether agree with you here. I am sure that if, at that time, you had consulted me as you are doing now, I should have given your problems just as much consideration, and that your mother would have done the same. Besides, if you will forgive my saying so, as a very old friend of the family, I think that it was hardly — shall we say? — an entirely honourable thing to take a step, of which you knew she would not approve, behind her back. I will say no more than this, because I am certain that you will have already come to look upon the matter in this light, and will have made her an apology. I know that at the time you acted on the impulse and did not consider what your action might mean to other people.

'Thirdly, about the writing. I think, myself, that this is an excellent idea and one which you should stick at. You will be able to find plenty of odd moments for it during the week-ends. I have always been sorry that I didn't go in for something of the sort, too. I used to have rather a taste for writing verses, in autograph albums and so forth. But I expect that you aim at bigger game! Well, it's a long job, and a waiting job, but there's plenty of good money in it. A man I know often makes as much as forty guineas month on stories he writes for magazines. It's just a matter of being able to spin a yarn, and knowing what will catch the public eye. He would be able to give you a lot of tips, I expect. If you like, I will ask you both to lunch and you can show him one of your *magna opera*. He is a very decent fellow and altho' very busy – he is a journalist and up most of the night – would, I am sure, find time to read and criticize it.

'And now, my dear boy, don't let yourself get depressed, and don't imagine that you have done anything so very dreadful or irrevocable. I feel quite sure that this bother can all be straightened out and put right, if we take it in time. Again I must say how very glad I am that you decided to consult me. As you know, your father was a dear old friend of mine, and there is nothing I wouldn't do for him or his. Indeed, I always regard myself as being, to a certain extent, "in loco parentis!"

'You will be wondering if this letter is ever going to end. I have made it such a long one because I wanted to go over the whole ground as thoroughly as possible. I think I have done so, but if there are any other questions you want to ask, please write again. I am always glad to hear from you at any time.

'Meanwhile, I will do what I can.

'Is Joan an accomplished cook yet? I must come in and taste one of her dishes!

'Please give my kindest regards to your mother.
'Yours very sincerely,
'ARTHUR LANGBRIDGE.'

·　·　·　·　·　·　·

84

Three days passed. Philip wandered idly about the house or sat reading downstairs in his room. He neither painted nor wrote. Mrs. Lindsay looked cheerful; Miss Durrant was using the sitting-room again. How much had she ever been told of all this? What jumbled explanation of events had she puzzled out for herself? She was used to being kept in the dark.

Nothing, apparently, had been settled or decided.

Philip went out that afternoon and returned late. He found a letter waiting for him on the hall table. Type-written. And read:

'Dear Mr. Lindsay,

'It has been represented to me by my friend, Mr. Langbridge, that there has been some misunderstanding with regard to your resignation on the 25th of last month.

'If this is so, I may say that I am prepared, on his account, to make an exception to my general rule and hold your old post open to you.

'I should be glad, therefore, if you will let me know your intention in this matter as soon as possible, and if you will come and see me personally either to-morrow or on Thursday.

'Yours sincerely,

'Harold Eliott.'

But Philip had no time then for more than a mere gasp; the next instant the sitting-room door had let out his mother who, ('can she have *steamed* it open?') radiantly smiling and with an extraordinary little prancing air of social animation cried:

'Oh, here you are at last? Come in, we've got a surprise for you!'

CHAPTER VI

THE new corpse, like most others, resembled Dante Alighieri. Eighteen of them were working on it, chattering in low voices, while the lecturer described the thorax to a group round one of the further slabs. 'I must ask you, gentlemen, particularly to notice – ' A skylight flooded the grey, stubble-bearded face with sunshine.

I was angry because I was startled; idiotic because I was angry. I was startled because I had been thinking about her when she appeared. I ought to get this clear. 'Honestly, though, that girl at the Piccadilly. The most amazing stuff she uses. Oh, God, no; I know Quelques Fleurs.' So early in Term, the smell was faint.

'Oh, I bet you. They all will, if you're prepared to do the thing in style.' Some people, it appears, take a morbid pleasure in having sold their bodies. In a little shop nearly opposite the gates, there lived a hairdresser who suffered from a most remarkable tumour. They wanted it for the Hospital Museum. He used proudly to tell all his customers. It was brought in last week. Time up at last. Allen slipped off his brown overall and shut the uncleaned scalpel with the other instruments in his case. Amidst general talk, he passed out of the dissecting-room into the lobby where they washed their hands.

Surely I could have known. Philip is right; I have no imagination.

In the students' club-room they played ping-pong, bridge, Charlestoned boisterously to the loud speaker. Young qualified men came in from the wards, wearing their white coats. Almost next door is the hut to which well-dressed girls go for treatment, limping.

Perhaps better wait till next week. If she is there this afternoon, am I prepared?

Allen went into the restaurant and chose his lunch at the counter. A cup of coffee, a bun, two sticks of chocolate. 'I'm afraid we're out of your favourite, Mr. Chalmers. But these are quite nice.'

That is exactly what would be worse than idiotic. The usual attempt to create significance. How I plot to make myself feel.

She may even expect me. No.

The little Mile End guttersnipe, already through everything but his finals, sat down at Allen's table and began to talk about work in the Casualty Ward. Interesting abdominal wound made by the hand brake of a car. Unreal to him as to me. But differently. My callousness is diseased. I half admired those men who fainted, last week, when we watched the operation.

The black-gloved figure intent over the white table. The room white and clean like a nursery. Remote as a child's sexual dream.

Between you, you didn't manage things very well. He starts to-morrow.

In her new shoes. For a minute I hated her like a boy of nine.

When she grins like that it would be rather nice to slap her really hard in the face. She'd hit back.

You're very smart to-day.

'A splinter of glass went in just under the collar-bone. Nothing at all. She was scared she was going to be marked for life.'

Am I? We're going to a tea-party. I'm meeting mother in Knightsbridge.

Her smile of frankly selfish pleasure. I lit a pipe.

Well, good-bye.

This annoyed her. Smiling:

Guess who with?

'Ever such a nice bit. Thanked me, twice. They have to have a nurse in the room, you bet. Chaperon.'

His grease-grey face, spotted. He sees what all wish to see, but is no nearer.

Yes. A mutual friend.

Near the bandstand, just beyond the trees. Haunted ground. I do love anything a bit classical. Artist, are you, dearie? Knew by your hair. These seats, far back in the darkness. Hat on my lap. Cheek to permanent wave. Deferred accomplishment of the already accomplished. These moments are the best.

There we stood.

Well, am I going? Yes.

I ought to have thought a bit. Smiled. Shaken my head. No, really, I'm afraid I haven't the very foggiest. All part of the game. Instead of blurting out. Red as a beetroot. Just as he would have been. Idiot. Idiot.

'Now just one little word of advice, my boy. Give it a rest, this week-end. You'll be all the better for it on Monday. Ta-ta. Be good.'

Right first time. However *did* you know? I know all sorts of things.

Whore's patter. When I was eighteen; selling French postcards by the Regent's Park Canal.

From the gate of the Medical School, Allen walked rapidly eastwards, under the long façade, to the 'bus stop. How would an ordinary person look up at those windows?

Whoever is in, I must make it perfectly clear that I've come to see Philip.

Until Phil told me afterwards, I never even realized that you and he – .

Spiteful this. I am not yet forgiven. Purely negative impulses.

So much to talk about. Boyhood's glory. At some tea-party I should enjoy reminding him, smiling. Almost the only time we ever spoke. Oh, surely you remember. Everyone listening.

The first summer at Camp. The field day.

Fancy his not mentioning that. You see. He's ashamed of me.

What the dickens is the rest of number five section doing over in that spinny? Another ten minutes and they'll be round our right wing. Lance-Corporal, will you go down at once and tell 'em to fall back like hell? I doubt if they'll manage it. That machine-gun'll get 'em as they cross the stream.

You've heard why?

We had killed an adder, and later smoked, playing dummy bridge in the ditch full of withered elm-leaves. He appeared, gasping, baby-pink, above the bank. I may as well tell you I shall have to report. Run away, little man; Daddy's busy. Privates Kelsall, Chalmers and Pepper failed for the second time to obey orders. In the tent, the Guards colonel was apologetic. I mean to say, it's hardly sportsmanlike of you fellows. This is after all more or less of a holiday. Extra fatigues; stolen fourth helpings of that metallic-tasting tea and fermented jam. Curiously enough, it was I who stopped Ronny putting wasps into his palliasse.

Philip didn't tell you that, too? What forbearance.

She looked surprised.

Surely, at least, I couldn't have; in that tone —
Like a young tripper I once saw in an hotel, who imagined that his wife had been insulted by two Oxford undergraduates. I suppose you two naturally despise me because I'm not a gentleman.

Oh, dear yes, I was absolutely dead drunk in the middle of the lounge. Crowded with spinsters. It must have been amazingly funny. You ought to have been there. You'd have appreciated it. I only wish I could have seen Philip's face. Unfortunately, I don't remember another thing until the morning.

Laughing in her face, shrilly, like a curate.

Our mutual friend carried me upstairs like a mattress. Shocked to the hair. You ask him about it as soon as you arrive. He doesn't believe young ladies have ever heard of such things.

Voice from the non-existent past. Ventriloquized through the lips of a pre-post-mid-Edwardian suburban clerk, sneering, with boils.

But I exaggerate. And for a purpose.

She said:

They oughtn't to have. I quite agree. And I shouldn't dream of asking him. If I'd been there I'd have kept you in better order.

Why can't you say frankly that you're shocked, too?

Blushing. A boy's quarrel with his governess.

Well then, I am.

Very much?

Terribly.

Smiling, absent-minded banter. Glancing for just an instant at her wrist.

You'll be late.

Oh, no. I'm in nice time now. I was early. Mind you come in and see us soon. Nobody wants to kill you. In fact, Mother hasn't even mentioned your name.

Merely to show you. Oh, yes, you amuse; when we can't find the cat.

This afternoon I'll puzzle them. By Christ, I hope he's there.

Calm. If my pulse isn't normal, I shan't ring the bell.

If he's there, she'll be watching us. And Philip. That'll be funny. How do you know? My special form of cowardice; taking attitudes towards things in advance.

·   ·   ·   ·   ·   ·   ·

The dust billowed down Bellingham Gardens; empty, bright. At the top of the steps, Allen stood waiting for the door to open.

I am perfectly calm. Prepared for anything. This visit has no particular importance. An old friend coming to a familiar house. Probably to be bored.

The snub-nosed maid:

'I'm afraid they're all out, sir. Mr. Page called for them before lunch in a car. I'm not sure, but I believe they've gone to the theatre.'

'Oh, thanks.'

It was quite warm. The bland sunlight had

warmed the stone beneath Allen's fingers. He would go for a walk in the Park.

'Miss Durrant's in, sir. If you'd like to give her a message.'

CHAPTER VII

JOAN had run up the steps. Had absurdly half-run, half-skipped all the way from the corner where the 'bus stopped. Pushing open the sitting-room door:

'Hullo,' she drawled, to conceal her lack of breath.

Yes, they were both there.

'Well, darling – '

'Well, dear. How did you get on?'

Joan gave her hair a shake and a pat in front of the mirror.

'Oh, not too badly.'

With a nervously careless gesture, she tossed her racquet into one of the chairs and sat down in another. They watched her, smiling. She was scarcely aware that she had begun to hum faintly, moving her heel.

'Have you had tea?'

'Yes, thanks. At the club.'

'What did you have?'

'I forget.'

Mary beamed.

'I suppose it's a most wonderful place.'

'Not particularly. It's quite decent.'

Her mother laughed.

'I'm afraid you're getting blasé, darling.'

Joan did not reply to this, but she flushed quickly. She had come bouncing into the room to tell them – what? Panting like a spaniel. Hullo Mummie. Hullo Currants. I'm happy. Hurrah. Phil would have laughed if he'd seen me. I am a clumsy great fool.

'And who won?'

'Oh, we did.'

'I *am* glad. I suppose Victor's a splendid player?'

'Not bad. I wasn't partnered with him, though, to-day.'

'Oh, weren't you?' Currants actually seemed disappointed. 'Then who – ?'

'I've forgotten his name.'

'Another young man?'

'Yes, of course.'

But all this fuss is humiliating. At my age. I wonder what that other girl would have said if she'd known. Which floor do you like best? The Empress Rooms or that place in Oxford Street. Luckily I guessed right –

'Tired, darling?'

'No, not specially.'

Another conscious pause.

'I think I'll go up and change,' said Joan, rising abruptly.

'Well ! She didn't tell us much.'

Mrs. Lindsay smiled.

'You're always in such a hurry, Mary.'

'The young people of to-day seem to take their pleasures so *sadly*. In our time, there was so much more enthusiasm. Still' – Mary sighed – 'I suppose it's all right if they enjoy themselves.'

'Of course they do,' said Mrs. Lindsay briskly.

Some moments later, she added:

'Shall you mind, Mary, if I don't come with you? I've got rather a lot of letters. And you know I don't really care very much for war films; although I'm sure this one will be wonderful.'

'Of course, Dorothy ' – Mary looked slightly bewildered – 'if you'd rather not. As a matter of fact, I don't know that I had any special intention of going to-night. There's all this week.'

'Oh, then I'm wrong. I had the impression that you'd particularly told me you meant to. But I daresay I imagined it.'

'No. I'm sure you didn't. Of course I must have said so. I'm getting very stupid. And I'll certainly go,' Mary hastily added, 'if it would be more convenient. I mean if you've arranged – '

Dorothy smiled.

'My dear! As if it was any business of mine.'

She began to turn over the papers on her bureau.

'Shall you be going to a Lyons; or would you like something kept hot for you here?'

'Oh, I'll have it out, of course, as I always do. I never want to make unnecessary trouble.'

'And we shall see you again about nine?'

'Yes, dear.'

Mary rose, with a barely audible sigh.

'Enjoy yourself.'

They kissed.

.　　.　　.　　.　　.　　.　　.

For nearly half an hour Mrs. Lindsay wrote, a faint smile upon her lips. She composed her sentences easily, without hesitation, but paused now and then to underline a word. She was not absorbed, however, in her work; for, at a small sound outside, she called:

'Is that you, darling?'

'Yes, Mummie.' Joan put her head in at the door.

'Were you going out?'

'Yes; just for a turn before dinner.'

'If it's nothing very urgent, I wonder if you'd be a pet and wait until I've finished this letter? Then you could slip it into the pillar-box on your way past.'

'Yes, of course.'

Mrs. Lindsay again busied herself in her writing, and Joan came into the room.

'Would you mind closing the door, darling? There's rather a draught.'

Joan did so and sat down. The letter was a long one. Presently, without looking up, Mrs. Lindsay remarked:

'I was hoping Victor would have come home with you. I suppose that now we shan't get another chance of seeing him.'

'Didn't I tell you, Mummie? He was leaving by a train at six. He had to dash off. You know, he ought really to have gone up yesterday.'

'Did he send any message?'

'Oh, yes. He asked me to say good-bye to you again. And to thank you again for being so kind to him.'

'It was he who was kind to us, I think,' said Mrs. Lindsay, smiling as she wrote.

In the silence, Time passed furiously, to the ticking of the silver travelling clock on the bureau. The Lindsays had taken it with them to Venice, on their honeymoon. Mrs. Lindsay's smile deepened.

'Of course, all these new ideas seem very strange to an old woman like me. In my day – well, it's

quite amusing to think what an unheard of thing
it would have been for a young man to take a
young lady about unchaperoned, after meeting
her five or six times.'

Rapidly underlining something, she added:

'All the same, I think we were much too strict
then.'

Joan said nothing.

'And, of course, his being a friend of Philip's
made it quite different. I never really thought of
him as a stranger.'

Those ghastly teas at the little shop on the
edge of the common, when they went down to
see Phil at his preparatory school. Two or three
of Phil's 'friends' were always invited. (At
least they were probably people he was afraid of
and wanted to bribe not to duck him in the
swimming-bath or gorse-bush him in the grounds
on Sunday mornings.) Mother used to ask them
all their Christian names, and call them by them,
as it were, in inverted commas. Now, Ronald,
some more cake? Dick, you're eating nothing,
I'm afraid. There they sat, crimson, like ugly
shock-haired mice in their huge Eton collars.
No; that was how she remembered them now.
At the time, they had impressed and terrified her
perhaps as much as they terrified Philip.

She said, with a perverseness unusual in her:

'One could hardly call him more than an acquaintance of Phil's. A friend of Allen's, perhaps.'

The smile left Mrs. Lindsay's face.

'Hardly that, dear, I should think.'

'Why not? They were at school together.'

'Well,' Mrs. Lindsay's voice was gentle but cold, 'I don't know; but they strike me as belonging to — shall we say, two different worlds?'

'Do you mean that Allen's not a gentleman?'

Joan was a little surprised at her own indignation.

'My darling, how you do snap my head off! Of course, I didn't mean anything like that. Only I was wondering what they could possibly have in common. Victor's so tremendously an open-air boy. So healthy and full of spirits. With, at the same time, such charming manners — '

'And Allen's unhealthy and dull and rude?'

('Heavens, I wonder what he'd think to hear me sticking up for him like this?')

Mrs. Lindsay smiled:

'You are absurd, darling. Of course, I know he's very clever.'

Still, since that queer meeting of theirs in the Park, she had the illogical idea that she was under

some sort of obligation towards Allen. That she
had, in an obscure way, behaved meanly to him.
So now, she felt she must continue:

'I know, Mummie, you think that Allen had a
lot to do with Phil's leaving the office. But,
honestly, I don't believe he had. After all, why
should he *want* Phil to leave? It did him no particular good.'

Mrs. Lindsay began writing again. Then she
said, with placid obstinacy:

'My dear, he must have encouraged him.'

'Well, perhaps; but that's hardly the same thing,
is it?'

There was another silence:

'I fancy Allen's fond of power. He'd enjoy
using his influence over anybody so very weak-
minded as Philip.'

'Really, Mummie; that is a little bit ridiculous.
Allen's got less ambition than anyone I ever met.
And Phil certainly isn't weak-willed.'

'Well, no doubt I'm wrong.'

The letter continued. Joan began to yawn impatiently. A step sounded in the hall.

'Hullo,' said Philip, putting his head in for a
moment.

'Well, darling. How did things go to-day?'

'As usual.'

Philip withdrew. When they had heard him climb the staircase, Mrs. Lindsay asked:

'Has Philip said anything to you about the office since he's been back?'

'No. Nothing.'

'I hope he's settling down. I think so, don't you?'

'No,' was the immediate answer on Joan's lips; but 'what's the use?' she reflected.

'I expect so.'

Mrs. Lindsay had finished now, and was re-reading her letter, making minute rapid corrections, very intently.

'You don't think that, while they were away, Allen could have told Victor anything about — that episode?'

'He might, possibly. But it's much more likely that Phil told him himself, if anyone did.'

'Oh, he would never do that.'

'I don't see why not.'

'Well, my dear, it's hardly — the kind of thing one boasts of, is it?'

'I don't know about boasting. I don't see anything to be ashamed of in it, if that's what you mean.'

Mrs. Lindsay blotted the first sheet.

'Let's put it, at any rate, that I should be sorry if Victor knew.'

'Why?'

'Im afraid it would lower his opinion of Philip. And I do feel it's tremendously important that Philip should be friends with people like Victor. He'll do Philip all the good in the world. I think he's got such a splendidly sane outlook.'

'The fact is, Mummie,' Joan grinned maliciously, 'you're getting quite a crush on him.'

Mrs. Lindsay flushed angrily; stung, and not for the first time, by the perverseness of her children. But she had plenty of self-control for such an occasion.

'Well, I must say this, dear. That I do think, I've felt it on several occasions, that you oughtn't to have taken all he did for us so much for granted. The time he took us to the theatre; it really was extraordinarily good of him. I don't yet feel quite sure that we ought to have let him do it. And afterwards I certainly thought you might have been a little more — '

'He's got heaps of money.'

'My dear — '

Yes, it was coarse; almost incredible. She murmured:

'I didn't mean that.'

Nevertheless, obscurely, she felt revolted by her

mother's tone. Need there be all this rubbing in of obligations, gratitude? Open-mouthed, goggling amazement because a young man from Cambridge chose to stand them stalls, tea with ices. 'But it's beastly of me to think like this. And perhaps Mother's right. I ought to have been a bit more gushing.'

Mrs. Lindsay folded the letter, put in into an envelope and handed it rather coldly to her daughter.

'If you wouldn't mind – '

But as Joan was at the door, she could not resist asking:

'Did Victor say anything more about Cambridge?'

'He said he'd write,' Joan answered curtly, and went out.

. . . .

Her walk was not a long one. For no sooner had she posted her mother's letter than she discovered a wish to go back and talk to Philip. Mrs. Lindsay's questions had made her aware that, lately, she had been neglecting him. 'I haven't been taking Phil seriously enough,' she thought. 'I behaved to Allen as though the whole thing had been a kind of practical joke.'

She found Philip in his sitting-room, reading.

106

Since returning to the office, he had, of course, refused, on principle, to paint or to write.

'Are you hating the place as much as ever, Phil?'

'Need we discuss it?'

'Not if you don't want to, of course. Only, I should like to know.'

Philip lit a cigarette, frowning.

'I suppose Mother got you to come and ask me this.'

'Phil. You don't really think that?'

'I don't know what to think,' his tone was pettish. 'I admit that I've quite ceased to understand the motives of anyone in this house.'

'Whatever do you mean?'

'What I say. I can't put it any plainer, can I?'

Joan asked, after a moment's hesitation:

'I – thought you liked Victor?'

'Have I said I don't?'

'No; but – it's something to do with him, isn't it?'

'Nothing whatever. Victor merely happens to be the person who's opened one's eyes to the fact that Mother's a sponger and a snob, if nothing worse.'

'Phil – I do really think – '

'Oh, yes, you're amazed. Naturally. Though I don't blame you to anything like the extent – '

'Blame me?' she laughed outright. 'What have *I* done?'

'Well, I must say, since you ask, I've got a bit tired lately of your persistent ingénue business. I fancy it bored Victor, too.'

Joan turned red. 'I'd enjoy giving Phil a good shaking, sometimes,' she thought.

'But, Phil, it wasn't in the least put on – my ingenuousness or whatever you call it. I'm afraid I was vulgar enough to be enjoying myself. I don't get taken to theatres and thés dansants and smart tennis clubs every day of the week. I daresay I showed it.'

'Yes; that's the humiliation of being paupers.'

'We're not paupers. Don't be silly. Heaps of people, much less well off than we are, go about and see things. It's only that Mother's been a bit old-fashioned, and she's got it into her head that since the war one can't venture outside the house. But she'd very quickly get over all that if we really wanted to do anything. Of course, we couldn't be as smart as Victor, but we could enjoy ourselves.'

'I suppose by all this you mean that I've somehow failed to do my duty as a brother?'

'All I mean is that sometimes – of course, I know you don't care much for dances or tennis or anything – '

'Really, I'm sometimes astonished at the sheer selfishness of your outlook. Isn't it enough that I've been hounded back into the office, prevented from doing my work, insulted by everyone in the family – ?'

There were actually tears in his eyes.

'Yes, I suppose I am selfish,' said Joan, half to herself. All Phil asked was to be allowed to work. Here was she, wanting – goodness knows what.

'And now I'm merely tolerated in the house because, at a hotel, I happened to make nodding acquaintance with Page. It's my one qualification, as far as mother's concerned.'

'I know mother likes him. But I think it's a good deal because he's your friend.'

'In that case, why doesn't she like Allen?'

'Oh, well – ' Joan grinned, 'as she was saying just now, he and Victor belong to different worlds.'

'So she discusses him? I'm asking him to dinner next Saturday, I may as well tell you.'

'I don't think she'll mind.'

'Mind? My God, if she does, it's time she gave me money to have my meals in a restaurant. I suppose,' Philip added, with a rather mischievous bitterness, 'that *you* like Victor because he's my friend?'

She flushed but met her brother's eyes smiling.

'Certainly not. I like him because I like him. Your friendship's no recommendation to me.'

'That's something to be thankful for, at any rate,' he grinned, in a better humour. 'Mind you, in moderate doses, I found him quite amusing, myself. He's got things in him you wouldn't suspect. Extraordinary. A kind of psychologic mongrel.'

She laughed:

'How immensely flattered he'd be to hear you say that.'

Sweet but penetrating, like theatrical church bells, the little tubular gong in the hall sounded for dinner.

As they were going upstairs, Joan asked, suddenly:

'Did Victor really say anything to you about being bored with me?'

'My dear girl, do you seriously imagine – '

'No, of course I don't, silly. I was only joking.'

Fool. Elephant.

CHAPTER VIII

'I say, I must be going. Look here, Page, which day can you come to tea?'

'Oh, thanks very much. I'll just consult my calendar.'

'Ah-ha. The famous calendar.'

Grinning, they all crowded round to look at it.

'Do you really put down everything? God, I like this. Work: two hours. Flics. Bike ride. Golf. Squash. Bath. Oh, but you ought to mention the House of Lords.'

'Lectures – surely they're the same every week.'

'No, they aren't. I may decide to cut.'

'Oh, my God!'

Yells of laughter. Slapping him on the back, they barged each other down the staircase, shouted up from the Court: 'See you in Hall. Tuesday at four. Don't forget.'

Victor crossed slowly from the window to his writing-table. Puffing hard at his pipe, he opened a box containing stamped college notepaper and envelopes.

'DEAR MRS. LINDSAY,

'This is just a line'

Nonsense. It wasn't. He tore the sheet up into little pieces and took a fresh one.

DEAR MRS. LINDSAY,

'This is to thank you most awfully'

Slang and too familiar. He crumpled it.

'DEAR MRS. LINDSAY,

'Thank you very much for the wonderfully'

Damn. Another sheet. Better make a rough draft of this.

First of all, what exactly do I want to say?

Is this – I beg your pardon, but does Mr. Philip Lindsay live here?

He does. But I'm afraid he's out now.

Oh, I see. Thank you.

He won't be very long, I expect. I'm his mother. . . . Won't you come in and sit down for a bit? It's so hot in the streets. You must be tired.

That's most awfully kind of you.

You must excuse my apron. I've been turning out some old cupboards. It's dreadful how one accumulates rubbish, isn't it?

'DEAR MRS. LINDSAY,

'I am writing to thank you very much indeed for all your kindness'

And so you're staying in Knightsbridge? Is that that gorgeous hotel on the left-hand side as you go up to Hyde Park Corner? I always think it must have such attractive views of the Park. And

all the horsemen in the morning. I do love colour
and movement. And the trees must be quite
beautiful just now.

'to me while I was in London.'

Oh, yes, of course you must have some tea. I
can't think where Philip has gone to. But he's
certain to be back in a few minutes now. And I'm
sure he'd never forgive me if I let you go away
before he came – Yes, and so you were saying. At
the hotel. I *see*. And you met like that. Won't
you have some of this cake? My daughter made it.
Yes, she has lessons. She's quite wrapped up in it
at present. So nice to have something regular to
do, isn't it? You're at Cambridge. That must be
perfectly delightful. Oh, I haven't been there for
years. Probably not in your lifetime! But before
I was married, I used sometimes to go there and
sketch. Oh, no. Very amateurishly.

I expect that's how your son gets his talent.

It's very nice of you to say so. But I'm afraid
he would have despised my poor little attempts.

'I haven't many friends there, and, naturally,
when my uncle had influenza, I should have been
left to myself if it hadn't been for your hospitality.
I'm afraid I made myself rather a nuisance to you.'

Now do tell me, because that's the sort of thing
a mother never hears – how does Philip behave

when he's on a holiday? Does he really paint the whole time? It's so amusing to meet someone who's been with him. I always enjoy talking to his friends. You'll think I'm dreadfully inquisitive.

'I wonder whether you and Joan and Philip would care to come down next week-end. It would be awfully nice if you could manage it. I can get you some rooms at the hotel nearly opposite this college and I would do my best to show you the sights.'

Ought Miss Durrant to be mentioned as well? He was still vague as to her exact position in the household. Was she a paying-guest; or a – didn't she? Philip had explained merely that she was an old school-friend of Mrs. Lindsay's. He had better mention her. She was rather decent; and it could do no harm.

Or no – he'd put:

'I wonder whether you'd all care to come down – '

That left them to fix it up as they liked.

My daughter, Joan. Well, darling, you're back early to-day.

.   .   .   .

The normal healthy boy does not worry very much about his soul. And perhaps he is

114

right. You will not make a plant grow in the earth if you are always digging it up to look at the roots.

Did you like it, honestly? I'm frightfully glad. That was Bach. By Jove, how ripping. Yes, I am most fearfully braced you liked it.

One can imagine nothing finer than that. Their heritage to us is, quite simply, in that memory. And as a young poet, who gave his life no less for England because upon a little lonely island, far off in the Mediterranean sea, has written —

And so this weakness, which at first seemed so pleasant and even harmless, will, unless you tear it out by the roots, grow and grow, until, at last, like some terrible cancer, it poisons your whole life. The hospitals to-day are full of boys, only a few years older than yourself; now hopeless, incurable mad-men.

Voices of the ghosts of the living.

Half-an-hour earlier, Victor was saying to his guests:

'Personally, I prefer *not* to think about it'; grinning amiably, nevertheless.

A member of the College Rugby Fifteen had picked up in someone's rooms a book. *Sex and*

Character. 'At the end of ten minutes, damned if I knew whether I was a man or a woman.'

'As far as I can make out, anyone who's got all these tricky complexes and what-not is about ready for a straight waistcoat; so why worry?'

Specimen sitting-room of adult male extrovert. Observable tendencies to Narcissism and Claustraphobia revealed by four team-groups, two Hockey, one Football, one Cricket and by the leaving open of both windows and the bedroom door. Motive for wearing tennis-shirt open nearly to the waist; probably exhibitionistic. Silver-framed photograph of Mrs. Page, taken a year before her death. (Mater Imago?) Undeniable traces of Compulsionism (particularly the excessive number of entries on the wall calendar). This last, however, had been noticeable in various manifestations since the age of puberty.

At fourteen, a story of Colonel Lawrence decided Victor to do exercises twice daily with his uncle's iron dumb-bells and to sleep every night of the holidays on the bedroom floor. This vow was written out, signed and afterwards burnt. Six months later, fag in a prefect's study, he turned the tablecloths every morning and reversed the chair cushions. When confirmed, he attended chapel Communion on alternate Sundays; and, being once caused by illness to miss, waited another fortnight. On receiving his cricket house-cap, he gave up for ever his favourite peppermints.

'But, according to this man, practically everybody has got some ghastly secret, which he can't remember; and until he does, it's mucking up his life.'

'In that case, I hope I've remembered mine and forgotten it again.'

Basley had been the first to notice. Jolly good innings, Page. That catch was rotten luck. But wait for them. I'm going to give you a place on the House side. They walked to the Grubber. Oh, go on, man. What'll you have?

'I know what Tom's secret is.'

Met next Sunday in a lane. Both blushing. Basley talked very fast. After this, encounters in the School Yard, in corridors, on the fields. Other walks. He liked people to notice. Hating it at the time; bored, embarrassed.

'I once had to go to a lecture in the Parish Hall. Some worthy on Auto-Suggestion. There's a good deal in it. Useful when you're listening to Sermons.'

Until, one evening, in the dormitory, they all began. Oh, yes, we know. His little friend. My God, I've been a fool. What stung, though he couldn't guess it, was that they hadn't. Nothing. I'll tell him to-morrow. Like two girls.

Miscarriage of their discussion precipitated the usual afterbirth of Boat Club limericks. Victor had a new one.

'You dreadful man. Phew. I'm off. Come and get some fresh air. My God, Page. I thought one drew the line somewhere.'

      I can't understand. You needn't try. I know what you wanted, now. And I never want to speak to you again.

.   .   .   .

'You haven't really seen Philip yet, at all. Come to dinner to-morrow, if you've got nothing more important to do.'

He glanced at Joan. She was looking out of the window. Next day, Victor bought a new shirt, pale grey silk, and a new knitted silk tie. None of his old ones satisfied him. He also shaved twice. Once was barely necessary.

She looked at the tie several times. He could not be sure whether she had or had not raised her eyebrows slightly.

After dinner, Victor was shown an album of

snapshots taken of the family at all ages. Joan had been a serious podgy child. She pointed out particularly hideous pictures of herself in gym-costume or old-fashioned bathing-dresses. It was like a confession to him of the whole of their past lives. Philip, who seemed in good form, supplied most of the comments:

'That's mother when the bathing-machine man had charged her too much and she called him a swindler and he threatened to fetch the police.'

'Really, Philip, what a dreadful libel!'

'That's me. At the end of the breakwater. I remember that was the day I stole an apple at the greengrocer's. And for months afterwards, I was terrified that I should die in the night and go to hell.'

'There's Currants, riding the donkey. Just before the saddle came off.'

'They call me Currants,' interpolated Miss Durrant, beaming.

Victor had nothing to say to all this. Linger-ingly, but with a certain impatience, he turned the pages recording September fortnights at Bognor, New Shoreham, Folkestone. Bad weather, lodging-house food, scoldings, haggling over bills. He was jealous of all those days. Yes, actually. He wished that he had been there.

School photographs followed.

'Do you play hockey, still?' he asked her.

'Oh, no. Nothing of that sort, now, worse luck. Now and then I get a game of tennis at a friend's house.'

'Don't you belong to a club?'

'No.'

'Oh, but you ought to. I've got quite a decent one.' (Had his voice been so patronizing?) 'Just for odd times when I'm in town – I say, that is if you'd care to, we might go over there one day and have a game.'

'I should love it.'

He fancied that her smile questioned him. He felt a stranger, an intruder; scarcely introduced. Philip and Mrs. Lindsay were most cordial. Both already used his Christian name. She evaded it.

That afternoon, the club was almost deserted He had never known it so before. At first, they had even to play singles. Mrs. Lindsay watched. Joan was disconcertingly good. Giving her one game was enough to make the set close. Towards its end, they reached deuce, changing advantages followed, and, becoming confused, she called the score wrongly. He let her cheat him, and lost.

'What's that scarf you're wearing?' she asked, later.

'It's the colours of the House I was in at school.'

He imagined her tone disparaging, and hastened to add:

'It's beastly, I think.'

'Do you? I rather like it.'

And the scarf wasn't really a bit beastly. He had always liked it himself. If only he had stuck to his own honest opinion, instead of making himself look a fool.

After tea, they were discussing the play. Victor reminded her of the set she had won. She gave a sudden ironic look, full in his face.

'Did you think I'd cry if I lost?' she asked, smiling. 'Yes, I noticed the mistake a minute afterwards. It was very polite of you. But please don't do it again.'

Was she ever likely to forget that?

And when he asked them to tea at the hotel, Mrs. Lindsay kept saying how grand everything was. It made the place seem vulgar. Joan had no comment; but, on another day, when they were dancing together, she said:

'You know, I envy you.'

He asked, what.

'All this.'

Probably she thought him idle, luxurious; a species of 'lounge lizard.' He explained with emphasis that he detested this kind of life, hated being in London at all. She appeared puzzled.

'Then why do you come here?'

He was dumbfounded at his rudeness. He trod on her toes. Apologizing:

'I haven't danced for ages.'

'Neither have I.' She seemed expert.

If only she wasn't despising him. He talked, to impress her, of football, everything manly. In a House Match he had once had his knee cut open, requiring four stitches. He added, without thinking:

'I'll show you the scar, if you like.'

Her humorously deprecating glance round the crowded room made him sweat as if in a nightmare.

Great God, I must be mad.

.   .   .   .

Victor sighed deeply.

'DEAR MRS. LINDSAY,' etc. etc.

'I wonder whether you would all care to come down next week-end.'

Better say: 'Some week-end, soon.'

That'll mean that they certainly won't come for a fortnight, at least.

I bet she doesn't come at all. She'll make an excuse.

I expect they're sick of the sound of my name. It was most appallingly bad form to go there day after day like that. That's what I should say if I heard of anyone else doing it.

I haven't known her a month yet.

I don't care what they think. I can't wait a whole fortnight. And I can't make more of an idiot of myself than I've done already.

He prepared to fair-copy his letter, glancing up as he did so, at the clock. Fifteen minutes gone already of Stubb's Constitutional History. Thinking about Joan was another of those occupations which could not receive the wall calendar's official recognition.

.   .   .   .

'Well, good-bye. I hope you'll have a ripping term. And thank you most awfully again for everything.'

'I say, I hope I haven't bored you dreadfully.'

'Don't be absurd. We've all enjoyed ourselves. You don't know how you've cheered Phil up. He needs it. He gets so seedy and worried.'

She might, at least, he later felt, aggrieved, not have chosen that exact moment to drag in her brother.

CHAPTER IX

IT was June, and the air tasted of dust. The pale fresh scars of the plane-trees were grimy when the bark had peeled. Ice-cream sellers pedalled about the streets. The town smelt of offal and of cheap scent.

The typists began to appear in their summer dresses, wearing bangles on their bare arms with a handkerchief stuffed inside. This trick of carrying the handkerchief offended Philip. He disliked the way the bangle was embedded in the red pimpled flesh. He disliked the aroma of the girls' increased sexual vitality, their whispered holiday schemes, giggled anecdotes and the snapshots which they passed round for their friends' inspection. Philip was in a queasy mood. Summer disagreed with him, making him look paler and fatter. It brought out shadows under his eyes. He became irritable and unhappy. He made stupid mistakes in his work and was rude to the other young men. They were accustomed to his petulance and tolerant of it. He had been discussed and dismissed long ago as a queer chap.

On a particular evening, the office smelt of paint. Philip left it, feeling slightly sick, and scrambled on to the top of his homeward 'bus. It was nearly full. He had to sit next to a woman with a dirty baby. The woman had been shopping. Her parcels had dark stains of oozing greasy substances. The baby had a sore on the corner of its mouth. His fellow passengers were greasy and tired. Philip withdrew his leg as far as possible and sighed. The Thames gull, poised in serene evening, regarded swarming thoroughfares, the scarlet crashing piece of mechanism on which he rode. Alone. Penny tumbling through his worn grooves; an automatic slot machine. In silver wrappings, the chocolate, familiar day-dream, with a portrait in four colours: Percy Philip Bysshe.

Arrived in Bellingham Gardens, he paused before the gate of number 36, considering his home. It had been repainted less than a month ago. White. Pretentious contrast with its dingy neighbour houses. But there remained the stained-glass fanlight above the front-door, for which Mrs. Lindsay seldom forgot to apologize to visitors. 'It's the only beautiful thing in the place,' Philip often retorted.

He opened the front-door with his latch-key and was immediately informed that vegetables were being cooked in the basement. There was usually a smell in the house at this time of day. Sometimes it was a mutton-smell, sometimes a bacon-smell, sometimes an unspeakable rank stench produced by what the cook mysteriously called ' "burning a few tins." ' On the stairs there was a different odour, stealing and sour, observable after wet weather, which Philip thought was drains. And in the bath-rooms there was a suggestion of decayed lemons and of slop-water. The smells made him feel almost savage. He looked for somebody to vent his annoyance on, but the dining-room and the sitting-room were empty. He wanted to meet his mother and to say something violent to her. He imagined his voice very curtly saying: 'This house smells of stewed guts.'

The phrase was Allen's. And Philip had now a sudden desire for the company of Allen, user of curt, foul, trenchant phrases which cut like a surgeon's knife into the gross body of vague words and dreamy thoughts which oppressed him. He decided that he would see Allen that evening.

Philip sometimes declared that his sitting-room was haunted by a phantom leakage of gas. The round mark made on the ceiling by the old fitting was still there. And this evening he believed him-self distinctly aware of the doubly invisible, stale presence. Moving to open the window, he noticed that both legs had come off one end of the sofa. Probably the maid had knocked them slightly while dusting. They had been loose for months. It was of no use complaining. There would only be irritable enquiries, stolid denials and a foolish little quarrel. As usual, the women would blame him tacitly for the accident and would vent their feelings later in some trivial obstructive act. That night, for instance, his hot water would be forgotten or his shoes not cleaned. And if he mentioned it in the morning, his mother's ostentatiously weary enquiries of the cook and the maid would rebuke his selfishness in making a fuss. Thus were the tactics of their domestic guerilla warfare reduced almost to a routine.

So Philip thought, as he stood regarding the damaged sofa. It was like a ship just beginning to go down.

But he had not calculated on his reactions to Mrs. Lindsay's remark at dinner:

'What have you been doing to your Chesterfield, Philip?'

'Do you mean my sofa?'

Items in her drawing-room culture upset his patience in a moment. She laughed:

'Whatever you like to call it. The *thing* in front of the fireplace. It's broken.'

127

'So I saw. Somebody must have smashed it.'

Again she laughed.

'Are you quite sure that somebody wasn't you?'

'Quite. When I went out this morning, it was perfectly all right.'

'But nobody's been in since, except the maids.'

'Well then, they did it.'

'But Philip, how could they have? I always tell them to be so careful.'

'I daresay they saw one of my letters lying underneath it and lost their heads in the excitement.'

'Philip, you've absolutely no right to say such things against people.'

'No, of course not. Not when it's your precious servants. When you accuse me of breaking a thing, of course, it doesn't matter.'

'I wasn't saying that you broke it. I was only asking *if* you knew anything about how it came to be like that.'

'I suppose you think I bit the legs off like a mad dog.'

'Philip, that's not funny.'

'It wasn't meant to be. It's quite sufficiently amusing to hear you politely calling me a liar because I say that the thing was broken by the only people who've been in the room all day.'

Here Currants, who had been listening in great distress, put in:

'As a matter of fact, I went into your room this morning, Philip dear, to put back that book you so very kindly lent me. So it might have been me.'

He knew that it could not have been, that she knew it, that this was, in fact, one of her typical efforts to make peace in the family. And it was an effort not without heroism; since the cost of repairing the sofa would be serious enough for her. He said wearily:

'Oh, I expect it fell to pieces of its own accord. It was probably feeling the heat.'

Currants, anxious to soothe him, laughed heartily. Mrs. Lindsay, with pursed lips, strikingly resembled her son. Philip could not resist adding:

'At any rate, you needn't worry. I'll pay.'

The meal came to its end in silence. Mrs. Lindsay went into the sitting-room, followed by Miss Durrant. Presently, from below stairs, Philip heard his mother begin to play the piano. Grieg. He clenched his fists.

There was a knock at the door. It was Joan. Of late their relations had become gradually less intimate. They did not see so much of each other. She said now, with a certain embarrassment:

'Phil, have you any message for Victor? I'm writing to him.'

'Whatever about? Isn't everything fixed for next Tuesday?'

She coloured a little and murmured:

'Practically, yes.'

Joan's evasiveness, so foreign to her nature, annoyed Philip:

'What message should I have? Do you want me to send him my love and kisses?'

She smiled:

'Poor old Phil, you've had a tiring day. Why not come out with me for a 'bus ride?'

'I'm going out to see Allen.'

'Again?'

'I suppose I shall be ordered to stop meeting him soon. As he's the only sane person I know – It's nearly a week since I went there last.'

'Is it?' she was soothing. 'I'd forgotten. Mother was rather wild to-night, wasn't she? Let's have a look at the sofa.'

'Chesterfield.'

They both laughed and bent down to examine it; but Joan was still thinking of other matters. She asked, suddenly:

'You're not awfully fed up, are you, Phil, because you won't be able to get down for the dance?'

'Of course I'm not. I saw quite enough of Cambridge, last time. It's the most vilely over-rated place in the Kingdom. Never shall I forget my disappointment when Victor took us to the Backs. But what's the good?' He looked at her, half-impatient, half-amused. 'That's wasted on you.'

'Entirely. I think it's all perfectly beautiful.'

He laughed: 'There we differ!'

As the earliest tinges of sunset were deepening beyond the gas-works, and with the Scandinavian sunrise rapidly mounting in pedalled chords behind him, Philip left the house.

.   .   .   .

Allen's rooms were in a quiet disreputable street; two stories up. Knock four times. His landlady, a friendly woman in artificial silk jumper and patent leather shoes, opened the door.

'You're fortunate, Mr. Lindsay. This is the first evening he's been in this week. I expect he'll be glad of a bit of company.'

Half-way up the stairs, one looked into a little glass-roofed verandah or greenhouse; now the kitchen. Washing hung across the doorway on a string. A cistern gurgled from the floor above.

'I've brought you a visitor, Mr. Chalmers.'

131

Allen, sunk deep into a chair with an anti-macassar, was reading a medical text-book, with steady exhalations of pipe-smoke. A lock of black hair fell over his forehead, brushing one eyebrow.

'You look like Sherlock Holmes,' said Philip, settling down and helped himself from a box of cigarettes.

Allen let the book slide off his knees into the waste-paper basket beside him. He smiled dreamily. He seemed placid as a tortoise. His old tweed coat mingled with the faded browns of the Victorian furniture around him. His books, pipes and various belongings lay about the room, on shelves and cupboards, not disturbing the symmetrical arrangement of hand-painted vases, terracotta plates. The lodging-house might have been his home from childhood. Equally, he might have arrived there that afternoon.

'You know,' Philip remarked suddenly, 'I do envy you. I should be perfectly happy here.'

'Should you? I wasn't at first; I loathed it. Now I don't notice.'

'I wish I could stop noticing our house. No, there's no comparison; this place would always, at least, be genuine of its kind. Ours is a whited sepulchre – my God – with a Prussian Blue door.'

Philip paused; then broke out:

'Allen, it's intolerable. I thought I could stand a good deal, but to-day – everything's been absolutely *vile*, since the moment I woke up. My God, that office . . . you've no idea what it's like now that the hot weather's come. The smell. And those girls. Jabber, jabber, chatter, chatter, chatter. . . And then I get home, and at once we start – haggling like bloody fish-wives over that mange-eaten old sofa in my room. Somebody's smashed it. You'd think it was a priceless china vase the way they talk. . . And day after day, month after month, year after year, it's going to be the same. At least, it isn't, because inside six months I shall shoot myself or have a nervous breakdown and be stuffed into the nearest asylum.'

'It would be far better,' said Allen, 'if you tried gin. Just a thimble-full when you get back from the office in the evenings. It makes one so good-tempered. And nobody'll notice.'

'Your everlasting gin. When you've a practice, all the patients will die of drink.'

'Oh, if you want my professional advice,' Allen grinned provokingly.

'Well?'

'But you don't.'

'Yes, let's hear it.'

'All right then,' Allen's lips drew out to a slow smile. 'First of all, I should tell you, you smoke too much. Take to a pipe or stop it altogether. Your eyes are bleary. Secondly, you've got indigestion; and no wonder, if I'm to judge from what you ate the other day when I had lunch with you in the City. Soaked, stewed-up trash. And all these sugary puddings. Have steak and stout. I suppose you're fearfully constipated. Eat lots of fruit. Thirdly, you're fat and you take no exercise. What's more, you've got into the habit of thinking of yourself as an invalid. As a matter of fact, it's ages since you had your rheumatic fever, and, unless you get wet or overtired, you're not in the least likely to have it again. That is, if you keep yourself in normal health. If you let yourself remain in your present condition, you're liable to anything.'

'You've certainly caught the voice marvellously,' Philip interrupted.

'I should sound you, of course. If your heart was all right, you'd start playing tennis as soon as possible. Every evening. Joan would help you. We should have a lot of difficulty at first with your self-respect. You'd be doing something you were no use at, whatever. Very painful for a narcissist. There'd probably have to be a kind of school discipline. Treat you like a boy of twelve. It could be managed more or less privately. Just a few friends.'

Philip was listening to all this with rather a set grin.

'And in the mornings,' Allen went on, imperturbably, 'you'd do some exercises. Especially the stomach and breathing. With one of those patent exercisers. Very important not to overstrain. The boy's strength would be quite enough for you in your present state. Of course, if you could afford it, a punchball would be handy. Spar with it, first thing, in shorts and two sweaters.'

Philip laughed energetically.

'Really admirable. Oh, I can see you complete with silk hat, frock-coat and spats. You'll be wonderfully convincing.'

'Shall I?'

Allen's smile was thin-lipped, subtle.

'I can see your arrival in some little provincial town. The Young Doctor. Oh, have you met young Dr. Chalmers? They say he's simply brilliant. I shall try him with the maids. And you'll sit at bedsides and smile; and gain an enormous reputation by saying nothing and curing a supposed case of cancer which is really something else.'

They sat looking at each other, both slightly abashed. Allen was thinking: 'Whatever made me? It wasn't mere brutality. No. But how idiotic. And how pointless. What's more, almost anything I could say now would make it worse.'

This was cat-ice. Rather painfully, Philip began to cut some figures:

'You know, I shall always maintain that Medicine is the most contemptible of all the so-called honourable professions. Lower than the Church. Just. It's a nice question. A choice of flavours in hypocrisy. The scientific mystic is worse than the religious. Oh, definitely. I never believed in an all-loving, all-powerful God until I'd dissected a frog's stomach, etc., etc. And even if one doesn't go as far. You remember the scene in *Joan and Peter*. Wells can be an unmitigated cad. Health for Health's sake is just a parrot's echo of Art for Art's. As you suggested just now. These absurd food slogans. Oscar Wilde's lily has found its way back to the fruiterer and florist. I suppose there's a connection between Bunthorne in Piccadilly and the song about walking down the Strand and having a banana. The sort of thing Frazer would trace in an appendix to the Golden Bough. It might have been hoped that the exposure of Nachkultur would have squashed whatever survived from the Boy Scout Movement. But, of course, as a vent to the less appetising forms of sexual exuberance – '

Allen yawned deeply. Philip abandoned his sentence midway, frowning, as if with pique, but nevertheless relieved.

'I don't notice *you* going in for punchballs,' he could not resist adding.

'Why should I?' said Allen simply. 'My constitution was designed for vice. It stands anything.'

There was another pause. Philip remarked abruptly:

'Great excitement about Tuesday.'

'Oh, the College Ball. Are you going?'

'Me. God, no. *I'm* not wanted. Mother runs this alone.'

Philip smiled significantly. Allen made no comment. Their talk drifted over other ground. But when, an hour later, he started home, Philip was aware with a small warmth of complacent spite, that his few words had planted their sting. Allen, left alone, pulled the book on to his lap and lit another pipe.

'After nearly five years,' he thought, 'of deliberate insults, I've offended Philip for life, and by

137

accident. He may imagine he's forgiven me. But that's just the stupid sort of thing one never forgets.'

Both of them were right.

CHAPTER X

THREE telegrams had arrived.

Cambridge. 11.0. Return postponed wiring later.

Cambridge. 12.15. Expect return for dinner don't wait.

Cambridge. 3.0. Returning after dinner please please both stay indoors no cause for alarm.

. . . .

'It only means that they've just got Mother out of bed,' said Philip, being shown them on his return from the office. 'That's what it is. Those Balls last till five or six in the morning.'

'Do they really?' Currants was thrilled. Past forty, the small hours had not yet lost their romance for her.

'Anyhow, we shall have our dinner tête-à-tête for once.'

She beamed with happiness. Mistress of the house; in Dorothy's chair. If only it were hers for good. To come in each evening to her soothing, vegetable society — what a relief. When Philip spoke to her, she was always amused or interested. When he was silent, she did not make him feel, as his mother contrived to, that she was being neglected.

'How would you like it,' he asked jocularly, 'if we kept house together, all on our own?'

A proposal of marriage. What a gesture. Spectacular as incest. She adores me. And legally we could. It'd kill Mother.

Downstairs, they played jazz records. Philip gave her a Turkish cigarette.

'I hope I shan't have a dreadful headache to-morrow,' she gaily smiled.

'Of course you won't. Now then, what's this one called?'

'It's one I know?'

'You've heard it a couple of hundred times, at least.'

' "My Baby loves Spearmint" – ? No, don't tell me. I'm so stupid. I'll think again.'

She knit her brows.

Mother, of course, wanted them to be in to hear all the latest Cambridge gush. How beautiful the lights looked through the trees and how lovely the band sounded and how wonderful all the dresses (she'd call them dresses) were, and what a delicious supper they had. Oh, and probably, rather later, there'd begin leaking out various hints. I'm not so old as I thought I was. All the fun I've missed. And somebody's uncle, exceedingly tight. It's never too late to begin, you know. Tee-hee. Faugh. But I'll sit like a lump of pudding and not move a single muscle of my face; even if she swears she's been —

'Isn't that the front door, dear?'

'Yes, I think it was.'

Currants jumped to her feet.

'Aren't you coming up?'

'They'll find us down here all right.'

'Oh, but I must just — '

She had bustled out. Philip lolled back in his chair. He heard his mother's voice in the hall, very distinctly, so that he could almost see her, in her silk dust-coat, drawing off her gloves.

'Well, here we are; back at last!' and then:

'Yes, it was a splendid train. We got up in — '

The sitting-room door closed.

Yawning, Philip picked up a novel. He half decided to go upstairs to his bedroom and be free of them until breakfast.

About ten minutes later, steps came quietly down to his door. It was Joan. She had taken off her hat and outdoor things. She looked pale.

'Mother hasn't been down here yet?' she asked, hesitating.

'No. Why? Is anything wrong?'

'Wrong.' The word made her faintly smile. 'Oh, no. Why should there be?'

She walked, rather listlessly, to his chair and sat down on the arm with a small sigh.

'This room wants papering,' she said.

Philip glanced up curiously at her chin. She was looking at the ceiling.

'What was the Ball like?' he asked. The last question he had imagined himself having to put. Unwillingly.

'Oh, not bad. You were right about one thing.'

'What was that?'

'They didn't have any chocolate ices.'

Several minutes passed. Joan spoke suddenly:

'Phil, I want you to promise not to say a word until I've finished — '

.   .   .   .

'Wasn't it?'

'My dear, I am so glad!'

For the fourth time, they embraced.

'They're very young, of course. I said that as soon as they told me. I said I hoped they would wait. But they're quite ready to. Victor would like to finish his time up at Cambridge. Of course, nothing has been in the least decided yet. . . . It was all so tremendously sudden. The darling children seemed almost as bewildered as I was. It had, well, come upon them, as you might say, so very much out of the blue. . . .'

'But they're absolutely devoted to each other – anyone could see that. I suggested to darling Joan, when we were by ourselves, that they hadn't let the grass grow under their feet. "Why," I said, "it isn't three months since you first met;" and she said: "Isn't it?" Just like that! I expect it seemed to them as if they'd known each other for ages.'

'Ages . . .' murmured Mary, enchanted.

'Joan told me first, of course. . . . And then we went along to have breakfast with Victor. That had been arranged long before anything like this had been thought of. . . . You can imagine how I felt! And he was so sweet about it. I knew how difficult it would be for him to begin, so I said at once: 'My dear, Joan's told me everything . . . and you may call me Mother!'

'Oh, Dorothy, did you? How wonderful of you!'

'I did! And what's more, I told them that I must have dropped my handkerchief in the Court, and that I was going out to look for it. Victor, darling boy, wanted to come and help

me. He didn't see what I meant. So, in the end,
I had to wink at him.'

'Dorothy! You *winked!*'

The two school friends exploded at this into
fits of laughter, until the tears streamed down
their faces. Dorothy was the first to recover
herself.

'Aren't I a wicked old woman?'

'I think you're a marvel.'

'Darling Mary . . . I wish you could have
been there.'

'I wish I could.'

'And if you'll believe me, dearest Victor had
actually not thought of wiring to his uncle. Of
course, I made him do it at once. And what do
you think Colonel Page wired back? "Am satisfied if Mrs. Lindsay is." That was all! I suppose he'll write by to-morrow's post. You know,
I've only seen him once, for a few moments.
He was ill in bed most of the time they were up
here. But I've always felt he must be a most
delightful man. With a quiet sense of humour. I
do hope that now this has happened we shall get
to know him . . . I tried twice to get a trunk
call through to their house in Surrey. But,
unfortunately, he'd just gone out.'

'He's very well off, isn't he?'

'Oh, very – I believe.'

'So that, I mean . . . it will make things easier for *them*.'

'For the children? Well, naturally, my dear, from a material point of view, it must. . . But I have enough of my own to have married my daughter to a crossing-sweeper, if that had been suitable. And, in the same way, of course. . . .'

'Of course. . . .'

'I don't deny that money makes things much simpler. One's not a hypocrite. For instance, Victor hasn't yet decided on his profession. And I think he's very wise to take his time. But, of course, if he hadn't two – well, I'm not sure of figures, the darling boy insisted on telling me, but I hardly listened – anyway, a good deal of money of his own – However, as it is – '

'Everything's turned out beautifully.'

'It has indeed!'

Again they embraced. And Mary asked:

'But, Dorothy, you haven't told me anything yet about the Ball itself.'

'Oh, my dear, it was wonderful, wonderful!'

'I'm sure it was! And I want to hear everything. Tell me about the new dances, and what the girl's frocks were like. And do the young man wear any special kind of evening dress – I

145

mean, like they do at the Hunt Balls? And I want to know whether there were many celebrities there, and who you talked to – and danced with, and what you had for supper!'

'Well then,' Dorothy smiled luxuriously, 'I'll begin, shall I, at the very beginning? First of all – '

. . . .

Half an hour later, Joan and her brother came upstairs. They did not cross the hall quietly enough, and, as they turned the corner of the landing, the sitting-room door opened.

'Is that you, children?'

By mutual impulse they both stood still, facing each other, outside Joan's room. There was a pause. Their mother said:

'I must have fancied it.'

The sitting-room door closed.

Joan made a face, and put her arms suddenly round his neck. He felt several tears run down inside his collar. She was trembling.

'I am an idiot,' she gasped, smiling. 'It's only because I'm so dead tired. Good-night, Phil.'

Nevertheless, within a quarter of an hour, after a wash, she was in bed, quite calm, unable to sleep and rather ashamed of herself.

The day of her engagement, twenty-two hours of which she had already spent awake, was not yet over.

They had lunched at the hotel as soon as they arrived, and were afterwards to go on the river. Victor wanted to fetch the cushions first. She always liked a chance of looking at his rooms. They were very austere; the bookshelves full of heavy technical volumes and files of notes; the window overlooking the street through iron bars. His bedroom was like a cell. Mrs. Lindsay admired the staircase. It was partly Elizabethan. She went out on to the landing to examine the woodwork, talking to them through the half-open door. Joan was in front of the cricket group. He was just at her side. Without being able to move, she suddenly knew exactly what was going to happen.

'Is this you?' she drawled.

'Yes, there. On the left, at the back.'

Mother, outside, could hear every word. His kiss had scarcely touched her cheek, just by the ear. A second after, she might believe she'd imagined it.

'Come along. Don't let's dawdle about.'

The afternoon was brilliant, and the Backs were crowded with punts and canoes like a London

street with traffic. The water beneath the gleam-
lit arches of the bridges moved sluggishly,
trailing dark-tailed shadows. Beyond the arches,
sunlit spaces where the college lawns ran down to
the brink were gorgeous like a bed of flowers
with the dresses of the women. A scintillation of
talk and laughter and of banjo-strumming rose
into the pure sky fringed by the opulent greenness of enormous trees.

She lay back, watching Victor as he stood
erect, steering with the end of the pole and gazing
straight ahead, high above her. His lips were
slightly compressed, as, with small movements of
his wrists, he guided the punt in and out among
the crowd. The whiteness of his open shirt was
beautiful against his sun-burnt forearms and
throat. 'It's funny,' she thought. 'I suppose
he'll like me best this evening, got up like a doll.
I like him best as he is now.'

As he helped her into the boat, he had mumbled:

'Are you very angry?'

'Furious.'

She had smiled into his face, astonishingly
mistress of herself, although she was tingling all
over. She was possessed with mockery. She
laughed almost wildly at the jokes of other young

men who joined them for tea. More people were introduced. She smiled at Victor from amidst the crowd, seeing him grow more and more wretched.

'I suppose you think I'm a cad,' he found time to say, as they were leaving for the hotel to dress.

'Don't be silly.'

'You don't – '

She was gone.

Mother was walking about the bedroom, smoking a cigarette and humming to herself.

'I'm so excited, I can't sit down.'

The Ball began just as dusk was closing in. The fairy lights sharpened in the deepening blue of the air. The band moaned and blared from the striped marquee on the lawn that sloped to the river. From the bridge, one looked down into black sinuosities of water cut into eddies by the tassels of the willow.

'Why won't you let me tell your mother?'

'That you've kissed me?'

'No, no. That I want to – that is, I mean. . .'

'But, Victor, do you, really, want to *marry* me?'

'I suppose, from your point of view, it seems funny. You think I'm a hopeless sort of fool. I oughtn't to have the nerve to ask you.'

Later, she said:

'But why this hurry? Why should all this be settled now?'

'Oh, of course, if you like, I'll wait. Until you know me better.'

He looked ready to drown himself.

'Tell me,' she asked, on the way in to supper. 'Had you made up your mind beforehand to — do what you did, this afternoon? I want to know the truth, remember.'

He admitted it.

'That is, you counted on the result. You thought: Once that's over, I've got her.'

'Surely you can't — '

'Well then, what was it for? A bet?'

She thought, for a moment, that he was going to yell out something awful. In front of the mask-faced college waiters.

Their conversation, continued whenever they sat out, (while they were dancing he scarcely spoke,) developed, as the night wore on, into an argument; and from an argument into a semi-quarrel. Victor became sullen between his outbursts. He seemed to have an uneasy longing to do something violent. Once, when they were standing together on the bridge, her handkerchief, a thing of no value, fell into the water.

'You'd better dive for it,' she said, laughingly.

And, to her consternation, he jumped eagerly on to the stone parapet. She restrained him with laughter, pretending that she did not believe him to be in earnest. But privately she feared that he must be drunk.

Then, at length, at about two o'clock, when the best of the night was over, and a chilly wind was springing up over the meadows before dawn, he exclaimed suddenly, in an absurd, desperate, peremptory tone:

'The point is – do you or don't you care about me?'

At last, he was moving. She said:

'My dear, haven't you any eyes?'

.   .   .   .

From breakfast-time onwards, both in her mother's presence and alone with him, she had been as cold as a fish.

CHAPTER XI

'I've got some news for you, darling.'

'What is it, Mummie?'

The crested envelope. From Victor. 'But to-day I'm going to try to behave absolutely naturally,' she had determined, while dressing. And already Currants had been fussing over her bacon and coffee, looking at her and speaking as though she were a case of nervous breakdown.

'I'll give you three guesses.'

She grinned teasingly at her mother.

'You've heard from that stout little man who danced with you.'

'My dear! No. . . .'

'Phil's been made manager of the business.'

'I'm afraid not.'

'Victor's changed his mind,' Philip supplied. 'He won't have her.'

She smiled across at him gratefully. This, intentional or not, was assistance.

'We give it up.'

Mrs. Lindsay was delighted.

'Philip's nearest. And even he, I'm glad to say, is a long way from the mark. It *is* something to do with Victor.'

'Ah.' Currants made a pleased, expectant movement.

'He's coming here to-morrow, for a week.'

'To stay!'

'Yes. I suggested it after our lunch. You remember, darling, you'd gone up to your room to get something? It was to be our little secret. He couldn't tell me definitely until he'd spoken to his uncle on the telephone; and, as you know, we didn't get through. But he was to try again yesterday and let me hear as soon as he could.'

They looked at Joan.

'I hope you're pleased, darling?'

'Yes, of course.' Faltering in spite of herself, she bit her lip. 'But are you sure – I mean, does he really want to come?'

'My dear, what an extraordinary question!'

A moment later, it seemed so.

'I only meant – ' she began feebly.

Philip glanced at his watch, and, getting up, strolled round towards the door.

'Let's have a look,' he said, holding out his hand to his mother. 'I want to see what sort of a letter Victor writes.'

She withdrew the crested envelope slightly.

'I don't know whether Joan would like – '

His good humour vanished.

'Heavens; you'd better get an Ark of the Covenant to keep it in!' he exclaimed, going out and slamming the door before anyone could speak.

When the unpleasantness of this had a little subsided, Mrs. Lindsay said briskly:

'But how we shall be ready for him in time, goodness knows. The house is in a dreadful state. We'd better start at once.'

'Where will he sleep?'

'Oh, naturally, in the front room.'

'But what shall we do about sheets on the big bed, dear? The other set are at the wash.'

Details were discussed. Joan got up.

'You're not going out, darling?'

'You know, Mummy, there's a morning class at the school to-day.'

'Oh, but need you go? You'd better put it off. Send them a note and tell them that you won't be going any more, for the present. I want you to help us get straight.'

Joan agreed at once; but immediately she felt a perverse desire to attend the class, which usually bored her. There would be nothing to do at home. Mother merely liked to have people hanging about, while she made the arrangements. On other occasions, when Joan had wanted to miss a day for some special reason, she had objected: Oh, but darling, I think regularity is the whole

point. You're never able to follow as well next
time and the lecturer won't go right over all the
ground again just because you weren't there.

However, since this was what Mother wanted,
she set herself to bustle about as much as possible,
doing all sorts of quite useless jobs. At any rate,
she wasn't going to spend the day hanging around
the house and thinking.

When Philip returned from the office that
evening, they were still at it.

'You ought just to give your sitting-room a
little tidy-up, darling,' his mother told him. 'I
didn't like to touch anything myself, of course.
But you've left all sorts of messy old papers
scattered over the chairs and the table. It's
hardly quite fit for anyone to go into.'

Joan quickly interposed:

'I don't really see that it matters, Mummie. Victor isn't an old gentleman. He's seen Phil's sitting-
room already, so the harm's done. Besides, it's no
business of his what the place looks like. You talk
as though he were a sort of sanitary inspector.'

'Well, it's exactly as you like.' Mrs. Lindsay
shrugged her shoulders petulantly. She was tired.
But Philip mildly answered:

'You wait. When I've finished, Victor'll believe he's back at the Ritz.'

Again Joan was grateful to her brother. He seemed, for her sake, to be exerting an unusual self-control. Actually, Philip had had an amusing idea. It would be delicately ironic to celebrate this visit by a feat of scene-shifting, a change of décor which everyone would notice, except, possibly, Victor himself. He stood contemplating his sitting-room as though it were a new canvas. One ought to attempt a sustained genre. Myself four years ago: seemed possible – provided that he had kept those pictures. He began opening cupboards. Dozens of water-colour and pen-and-ink drawings slid out, mounted and unmounted. Crucifixion of a pony and two bears, done during his Goya mania, seemed worth exhibiting. Later, he found a portrait of King George the Fifth, a string-framed text: Blessed are the Meek; and some stills of Miss Betty Blythe as the Queen of Sheba.

Joan had gone up early to her room, but she could not stay there. At this hour of the evening, the cries of mating cats rose piercingly from the back-gardens. She decided to go for a walk. Thinking that she heard Philip outside, she opened her door to call him. But it was only her mother, carrying on her arm a bundle of towels to put in the various lavatories.

'We can't give Victor scented soap, can we? Do remind me to-morrow to get some more white curd.'

.   .   .   .

At lunch next day, Mrs. Lindsay was wearing her best dress, black and coffee-coloured. She had got out her gold lorgnettes and put on a great deal of powder. Miss Durrant was in Sunday blue. It made her look enormous.

Afterwards, they all stood about in the sitting-room; although Victor was not expected till four. Mere waiting, even for a train, had a physical effect on Joan. Now she felt quite sick. What an utter relief it would be when he arrived. She had really behaved vilely to him up at Cambridge. But that was because she was unsure of herself. Now she would be as nice as possible; put him at his ease at once. And do you know, Mother's been fussing about the house these last two days as if we were expecting the Prince of Wales. This morning, she was almost in tears because she couldn't find the spare-room cosy for the hot-water can. She's taken the curtains out of my room because she thought they were swankier. Oh, and at dinner, you must try not to laugh —

Yes, perhaps that was spiteful, but she was happy. Rather hysterically.

'Haven't you any sewing you can do, darling? It really must look strange, the way we're all standing up.'

.   .   .   .

At half-past three, the front door bell rang.

'Quick, darling, for goodness' sake, and tell them in the kitchen that we're not at home to anyone.'

But the maid was already in the hall.

'Oh, dear, how tiresome!' Mrs. Lindsay made a gesture of despair.

Mrs. Clive and Miss Oliver.

'But it's only Mother's extraordinary stupidity,' thought Philip, bolting down the basement stairs. 'She'll be delighted when she realizes what this means.'

Indeed, the stage could not have been more effectively set for Victor's arrival.

Mrs. Clive, from her chair near the window, asked:

'My dear! who's this tall and handsome young man opening your garden-gate?'

'Oh – dear me, I expect it must be Victor. He's a little early. You've never met him before?

158

Victor Page? As a matter of fact, he's come to stay for a few days. . . .'

'I'm afraid we arrived at an inconvenient moment,' said Miss Oliver, (long ago christened by Philip: The Rector's Delight), in her sing-song voice.

'Not at all. I'm most *glad* you should be here. . . I know you'll excuse me just one minute?'

They heard the door open.

'Well, Victor darling, here you are!'

'Hullo, Mother.'

They came into the sitting-room, followed by Philip, who had been on the look-out from below, and could not resist the promise of this social tableau.

Both their callers frankly gaped.

'Did you have a nice journey?'

'Oh, yes, ripping – thank you.'

'May I introduce – Mr. Page; Mrs. Clive. Miss Oliver?' Mrs. Lindsay smiled like a revolving lighthouse. 'Now, Victor, I expect you'd like to wash your hands? Will you show him his room, dear? And come down as soon as you're ready, won't you? We'll have tea at once. Joan, darling, would you tell them, please, downstairs? It'll save their answering the bell.'

When Mary and she were alone with their mystified guests, she added:

'I couldn't tell you to the children's faces: Joan and he are engaged to be married.'

'My dear!'

'But how wonderful!'

'Have you been keeping this a secret?'

'When did it happen?' etc., etc.

'All,' as Philip later told Allen, 'that was lacking, was a concealed orchestra to burst into the finale of "1812."'

. . . .

Mrs. Clive and Miss Oliver left as early as usage allowed. Mrs. Lindsay saw them to the door, was told that her future son-in-law was perfectly charming and supplied them with a few details which would, she knew, be communicated within two or three days to most of her other friends.

'Thank goodness they're gone at last,' she exclaimed, smiling, on her return to the sitting-room. 'I'm dreadfully sorry we let you in for them, Victor. It was quite unintentional. They *will* call here from time to time. Philip has some dreadful name for one of them, which I'm glad to say I've forgotten. But you'll soon get to know all our jokes, now that you're a member of the family.'

'My God,' thought Philip, 'what'd he think if she started treating him as one?'

Joan was looking at her lover. She took up her old question: what does he think of us, apart from me? What does he think of Mother, Currants, this house? Are they just tiresome extras given away with the packet?

He would never tell me, of course. Not even when they were married. She tried to picture themselves married. All was vague. She only saw symbols. An income-tax form. Slippers.

Her mother was saying:

'And you won't forget it's at seven-fifteen, will you?'

She realized that they were about to be left alone; and, with a shock, that to-night she would have to dress for dinner.

.   .   .   .

They sat for some minutes in silence. He seemed to have lost his tongue. She was annoyed to find herself nervous and fidgety again. 'The country house touch,' as Philip described their mother's social efforts, had shaken all her resolutions of the morning. She put her hands in her pockets, got up whistling and walked to the window.

She said:

'Shall we go out for a bit?'

'Just a minute ' – the nervousness in his voice reassured her – 'I've – there's this – I wanted you to see. . .'

He came round the edge of the sofa, holding something out. A little box. She stared rather stupidly at it.

'Opal. October is your month, isn't it? I – ' he laughed, awkwardly – 'looked it up in a dictionary, yesterday.'

'Victor, how sweet of you! It's lovely.'

She took it in her hand, held it to the light, admired it from every angle. He did not move. At last she glanced at him, with a nervous grin.

'It isn't just to look at, is it? May I wear it now?'

'Of course.' He blushed hard.

'Will you put it on, please?'

He jerked into movement.

'I hope it'll fit all right. Your mother lent me a ring she was wearing, which she said you'd tried on once.'

'You and Mother seem to have thought of everything, between you.'

Regretting immediately the faintly resentful tone of this speech, she held out her finger. They fumbled together clumsily. The ring dropped. He nearly trod on it. It was on.

'We ought to have been more graceful,' she said, smiling. 'It's a kind of ceremony. Now we're really engaged.'

He grinned, awkward, and stood looking at her. She did not wish he had more address. It even cost her nothing then to say:

'You can kiss me, you know.'

His step forward was tentative; but, at the movement, she was in his arms. And with passion. An obstinate triumph at the arrival of this moment, after the hours of delay, the chatter round the tea-table, made it almost exquisite. Several instants were mere blindness. Then she felt the pressure of his hand upon her shoulder grow limp.

She loosed her arms abruptly. Victor was scarlet in the face. His silk collar was rumpled. He looked half asphyxiated.

She flopped down on the arm of a chair and burst out, uncontrollably, laughing.

'I didn't hurt you, did I ?'

For a moment, she thought he was going to leave the house; but he walked slowly across the room, stood with his back to her, presently straightened his coat, and, turning again, mumbled that they had better start, or it would be late.

CHAPTER XII

PHILIP assured Allen that he was quite enjoying Victor's stay at Bellingham Gardens.

'One had foreseen, of course, the merely psychological interest; but what I hadn't realized was that there would be all sorts of unexpected decorative values. Rhythms, really. I keep seeing things I'm certain would appeal to a choreographer. It rather reminds me of that charming ballet (which they aren't doing this year, thanks to the new acrobatic trash), called — Oh, I forget the name, but there's the duenna and the young countess and the valet-de-chambre — you probably don't quite follow what I mean —'

What Philip vaguely meant was that Victor, when he came downstairs in the morning, kissed Mrs. Lindsay on the cheek; that he stood up whenever Joan moved from her chair and was ready to open the door for her when she left the room; that he called Miss Durrant, Currants, and held her skeins of wool; that he was at any time prepared to run errands or take letters to the pillar-box; that he generally slapped Philip on the back when they met, and always came down to Philip's sitting-room after dinner to smoke a pipe, tell a few limericks, or, more seriously, to ask, without borrowing them, what books he ought to read. Something decent, I mean. One gets frightfully tired of shockers.

'Hullo, Philip!' was his evening greeting. 'How's business to-day?'

'Not too bad.' Philip smiled blandly. 'My boss nearly gave me the sack.'

They didn't, of course, believe him at first.

Sit down, won't you, Mr. Lindsay?

One could not dislike Eliott; his manner was so nervous and apologetic.

To come straight to the point, your work of late has not been – well, entirely satisfactory.

I'm sorry, sir.

There had been a polite pause.

Well, what about it? Can you suggest any reason?

No, sir.

I am sorry to hear that. I had hoped that you would have been able to help me.

Not sarcasm, this.

You haven't been feeling unwell because of the heat?

No, sir; not especially.

You are quite satisfied with your position and duties here?

Quite.

Perplexed. Carefully parting and joining the finger-tips of both hands.

Some months ago, for reasons which you did not, at the time, see fit to give me, and which I will not ask for now, you gave up your post in this business. Later it appears that you changed your opinion as to the wisdom of that action. Might I enquire whether you are on the point of changing it for the second time?

Oh, no, sir.

Very well. I see. I am pleased to hear you say so. . . . Then perhaps you will not mind my suggesting that, in future, you might see your way to – er – how shall I put it? . . .

Perfectly, sir.

Good. Then I need say no more. We under stand each other. . . . And now, Mr. Lindsay, I won't detain you any longer. Good-night.

Good-night, sir.

Poor Mr. Eliott. Probably he had gone home to his villa and four children and loud speaker on Putney Common and had worried for the rest of the evening as to whether he had or had not been fair to his employee.

'Well; you'll have to mind your p's and q's for a bit.'

'I shall, shan't I?'

Philip joined loudly in Victor's laughter. His mother's lips tightened.

'By the way,' she said presently, with an air of complete inconsequence, 'we ought to ask Mr. Langbridge here some day soon. We haven't seen him for ages.'

Dusting the whip. But Currants, as usual, spoilt it all.

'Surely, Dorothy, you told me yourself, not long ago, that he'd gone on business to Germany for the rest of the summer?'

'Did I, Mary? I really don't remember.'

Presently Joan joined them downstairs.

'I say, Phil; it was true what you said just now, wasn't it, about Mr. Eliott?'

'Of course it was.' Philip felt some misgivings in thus taking Victor behind the scenes; but she, evidently, did not. 'Did you think I was just getting at Mother?'

'I wasn't quite sure,' said Joan; and added thoughtfully: 'It did get her, didn't it? She'd be furious if anything went wrong at the office.'

'Oh, yes; she'd be furious. But what would she *do?*'

Philip began to pace about the room, jingling pennies. He felt suddenly excited, triumphant; something was going to happen. He was at the centre. Victor, after all, could only watch him, smoking his pipe, looking mystified.

'She couldn't get me into another one. Not if I'd been sacked for incompetence. Not even Langbridge in all his glory could do that. I should have to take up some other profession – be a 'bus conductor or a Member of Parliament or something – '

Victor guffawed.

'I can see you as an M.P.'

'But should you like that any better,' asked Joan seriously, ' – just another job, I mean?'

'Of course I should. And really, almost *any* other job. Because this one is certainly exceptional. You know, a boy of fourteen could do the things I have to. The first year, it was mostly licking on stamps and sorting letters. No, I'm wrong. Sorting letters was a privilege. I didn't rise to that until my second year. And even now – One doesn't need the initiative of a gnat. A crossing-sweeper at least has to dodge the traffic. It's more exciting.'

'But, Phil, in time you'll have to do important things, won't you?'

'Yes; if I'm a very, very good boy until I'm thirty-seven. It's one's *life*, this; mind you. Year in, year out, I'm to be cooped up in this place until I'm only fit to retire and be buried.'

'It must be a jolly rotten sort of existence.' Victor was impressed.

'Not for everyone. Do you know, most of the people in our office thoroughly enjoy it? Yes, it seems hardly possible, but they do. And the rest, though they'll grumble, are quite contented. That's just it. I'm almost certainly keeping out some unfortunate young man who'd actually *like* to be in my place. They think I'm crazy, you know, because I want to do something which requires a little doing, and because I occasionally seem to need fresh air.'

'Good Lord,' Victor was becoming quite indignant, 'they must be a wretched kind of a gang. I'd no idea – '

'No, that's exactly the point. Most people imagine that offices are full of public school men. Hearty sort of places' (this was playing to the gallery with a vengeance; but where, after all, were the circle and the stalls?) 'As a matter of fact, that's sheer bluff. You'll find them in partnerships; yes. A few go in from the bottom and do well; then, of course, it's advertised. Most can't stick it, and clear out abroad. The spade work has got to be done by the regular clerk type. A navvy wouldn't dirty his hands with it. He's much too independent. To be any good, you've got to love your little rut and be deadly jealous of all the other people in it. The queer thing is, though, these people haven't a desire to get rich. They've lost even that. One of them said to me, a few days ago: "I'd like to see Oxford and Cambridge burnt to the ground. I would. What do they turn out but a lot of snobs and wasters? Nobody ought to be allowed by law to earn more than eight hundred pounds a year. Not more than four hundred pounds, till they're thirty-five. If I can live on that, then other people can." '

'God,' said Victor.

There was no doubt; Philip had been impressive. Joan was watching her lover's face.

'And then, look at it in another way. This is a whole-time job. A whole-life job. Well, put aside everything I've said so far. Imagine it absolutely perfect. It's still a job for somebody who's got nothing else they want to do. I have. I want to paint and write. Of course, I see now that Mother would never allow me to do that and nothing else. But if only I had some work which gave me time for other things as well, I'd be quite contented. I do think I ought to be allowed that.'

'I should jolly well think you ought.'

'Mind you' – they were all moved, now. Victor, generously stirred; Philip, pleasantly dizzy with eloquence; Joan, excited by her brother's success. It was no time for caution – 'it's only fair to Mother to admit that I did set about it in the wrong way. I don't know whether Joan's told you anything – but you may as well know now that there was a silly incident last Easter. When we met you, in fact. Things had come to a head then; and I'd simply walked straight out of the office. I couldn't stand it any longer. It seemed better at the time than making a lot of fuss and unpleasantness at home. And, you see, by doing that, Mother had absolutely no responsibility for it. I took the whole thing on to my own shoulders – '

'I say, really? Had you, then? Do you mean you'd cleared out – ? '

'Of course, I don't defend it. It was really rather cowardly of me, I suppose.'

'Cowardly? I don't see that, at all. I don't know. Personally, I should have thought that – under the circumstances – it was rather a sporting thing to do.'

'Oh, well. Anyhow, it's done and over, now. When I got back, Mother seemed so upset that, of course, I simply had to let myself be shoved back into the place again. It all seemed rather futile, but I don't know that one could have behaved any differently. Argument's no use. And there wasn't any other job handy at the time. There isn't now, for that matter. If Mother discusses the subject, she just says: "Well, you can do your painting and writing in the evenings and on Sundays." She doesn't realize that the evenings are ruled out for painting except during about two months of the year; and that I'm always feeling too tired, after being in that stuffy atmosphere all day, to do anything serious. If I'd come in from a day in the open air, it'd be an entirely different matter. My brain would be fresh, at any rate.'

Thus Philip continued; his argument describing several more circles, parabolas.

As they went upstairs to the sitting-room, leaving him reading a novel, Joan pressed Victor's arm.

'I'm awfully glad you agreed with Phil,' she said.

He was surprised and amused.

'Did you think I shouldn't?'

'Well, no – not exactly. But I'm glad you did.'

Victor laughed.

.   .   .   .

173

Much later that evening, Mrs. Lindsay told them that she had still some letters to write. They weren't to bother to stay up. Currants left the room, obediently, at once. And Joan and Victor soon followed her. As they said good-night, Mrs. Lindsay asked:

'Would you, darling, just bring me down my little bag? I think I must have left it up in my bedroom.'

Victor, of course, offered to take it, but Joan said:

'No – I think I'd better.'

'Thank you so much, darling. . . . Oh, while we're together, I just want to ask you something.'

'Yes, Mummie.'

'You heard what Philip said at dinner about the office? Of course, I know he was exaggerating, as he always does; and we understand him. But I want you just to point out, as you can so much more tactfully than me, that he really must not discuss these affairs in front of Victor.'

'But, Mummie, why ever not?'

'Because he might so easily misunderstand the whole situation.'

'Then surely, the sooner it's thoroughly explained to him, the better.'

'I don't see why he should ever know anything about it, my dear. It's been extremely unpleasant to me; and I'm sure it would seem so to him.'

Joan indulged in a rare moment of irony.

'You yourself said the other day that we were going to treat him as a member of the family.'

Mrs. Lindsay ignored this.

'And, darling, I'm sure you can make Philip see that this is not fair to yourself.'

'To me!'

'Certainly it isn't.'

'I don't in the least follow –'

'Let me put it in this way. If Victor gets this unpleasant and quite wrong impression that Philip seems so extraordinarily anxious to give everybody of himself –'

'Mummie, if I thought that Victor disapproved of anything Philip had done –'

'Darling, I've always tremendously admired your loyalty; but you really must face the possibility now, that if, let us say, Victor did discover everything that has happened, he wouldn't at all –'

The temptation to refute this, triumphantly, in four words, was very strong. Joan's gratitude to her lover increased proportionately. But years of dealing with her mother had taught her prudence. She was silent, and Mrs. Lindsay added:

'You see, my dear, this is all so profitless, as well as being unpleasant. What does it lead to? I know, of course, that Philip's a little done up with all the hot weather, but he should try to be more controlled, and think of other people's feelings. Of course, one realizes that the work is a grind. But then, life's a grind. We must all buckle to and do our share. One can't expect it to be one long holiday.'

(Joan, at this point, irrelevantly remembered how Phil had once, in architectural jargon, described their different modes of conversation: Currants' is Early English, Mother's Decorated and Allen's Perpendicular.)

'I know you'll catch me up again and say that I'm prejudiced. Well, perhaps I am. But you can't deny that Philip's been seeing a good deal of Allen lately. He makes no secret of it. . . . Of course, I should never be so absurd as to forbid his going. But I do think that if you could try to amuse him more in the evenings – Get him to come up here and sit with us. Naturally – while darling Victor's in the house – I quite understand that you two want to be together; and he's been wonderfully good to Philip. But when Victor's gone. If only you could lead his thoughts away from all this discontent and misery.

I suppose it's the effect the War's had. Your
father was such an exceptionally happy man. . . .
And then Allen fills his head with all kinds of
absurd, unwholesome ideas. I don't think Allen's
mind is at all wholesome. I don't blame him
altogether, poor boy. I expect he has a very
lonely life, living up here in town, away from his
parents. I think Philip said once that his father
was a clergyman, didn't he? And then there's
his profession. This constant brooding on diseases and death must be very bad for anyone who
hasn't a tremendously healthy, sane outlook on
life to begin with – '

'But, Mummie, you talk all the time as though
Phil hadn't anything definite to complain of, or
anything that he wants to do – '

'Oh, my dear. Don't imagine that I've forgotten all the talk we had two months ago. I never
shall. But what did it amount to – ? Philip
wants time to write and paint; well, he's got all
the evenings, and his week-ends. Do you ever
see him doing anything then? In the past he
used to, I admit. And in the past we didn't
have so much of this talking and complaining.
By all means let him paint, if he wants to. I
think it's a very good thing. It takes his mind
off all these imaginary troubles.'

'But,' again it was on Joan's tongue-tip to refer to the earlier conversation. Instead she asked : 'You *can't* call them imaginary – ? '

'Well, all I *can* say is that Mr. Langbridge, who's got all the experience of City life behind him – '

'Oh, Mr. Langbridge – ' Joan broke out, with bitter impatience; 'he's old.'

'My dear, he's two years older than I am.'

'I'm sorry, Mummie. I didn't really mean it like that.'

There was a pause in the conversation. Mrs. Lindsay felt as though she had noticed, just in time, that she was about to sit down on a wasps' nest. All kinds of stinging things might have come out of it. Meanwhile, Joan's uppermost feeling was that she ought, in fairness, if not to report some of Philip's words, at least to warn her mother. She said:

'Mummie, have you ever thought what Phil might do if, well – if the office got too much on his nerves – ? '

'I hardly see what he could *do*, my dear.'

(The coincidence in phrase startled her.)

'I mean, supposing he lost his job – after what he told us this evening – '

'My dear, I think he'd be careful not to do that.'

'You remember what happened at Easter.'

'Certainly I do. That's why I say it. It was all very fine to try that sort of thing once. But twice wouldn't do. Mr. Langbridge wouldn't be able to get the post back for him again. And he'd hardly care to bother much about Philip's future after such an insult.'

'But, Mummie,' Joan persisted, biting her lip, 'just supposing that Phil got really desperate. He might leave home too, this time.'

Mrs. Lindsay smiled primly at her daughter's earnestness.

'What would he do then, I wonder?'

'Oh,' Joan was getting impatient, 'he'd find work of some sort to do, of course.'

'Would he, darling? But you can set your mind at rest on that score, I think.' Her mother's tone was soothing, indulgent. 'I fancy you'll find Philip is very fond of his comforts. He wouldn't give them up as easily as you imagine.'

Philip came in through the slightly open door. Noiselessly. He was wearing bedroom slippers. But it was Joan who started, not Mrs. Lindsay.

'I thought you'd gone to bed hours ago, darling.'

'Phil, were you looking for your wrist-watch? It's here. You left it on the mantelpiece.'

He put out his hand, but his eyes were upon their mother.

'You shouldn't talk so loud,' he said. 'As I came up the stairs, I heard every word.'

He left them, blankly standing. Mrs. Lindsay looked foolish; but Joan was really frightened. She had, for the first time in her life, seen hatred on her brother's face.

CHAPTER XIII

WILDLANDS, the latest home of Victor's restless uncle, was the Victorian red-brick substitute for a country house, approached by lanes scattered with fir-cones and pine-needles, through woods surrounding the lower slopes of Hindhead. The building had two wings; one, a billiard-room. Colonel Page had knocked down the other and built it up again as a covered squash court. He had also felled a good many trees. But the garden remained a forest clearing; the atmosphere was resinous, oppressive. The ensign, limp upon the tall white flagstaff in front of the house, was distinctly reflected in the green dark lake. The water had the greyish greenness of the surrounding pine-trees. And the pines and the bright rich colour of the sandy earth made the delicately tinted roses on the pergola look false as crêpe.

To Joan, the whole place seemed rather sinister. She had once nearly trodden on a snake, coiled up just outside the dining-room window.

Colonel Page invited her and her mother down to spend a week, soon after Victor had left Bellingham Gardens. Mrs. Lindsay was delighted. She failed or refused to notice how Colonel Page avoided her company. And, indeed, his rudeness could scarcely be considered offensive. It was quite impersonal. He had merely no use for middle-aged women. Of Joan, he seemed to approve. He was anxious that she should learn to ride.

She found interest, as Allen had done, in the relations of uncle and nephew. She could imagine, now, their life alone together; their games of squash, their pipes, their monosyllabic conversation: (Off now. Town? Yes. Car? No.); and then the hours when Colonel Page shut himself up in his study; and Victor was left to himself, to drive to London or the South Coast, go for a gallop, invite people to tennis. Plenty of young men and girls, their neighbours, came to the house while she was there. On these occasions, his uncle was seldom seen.

'I say, Joan, what a ghastly bore. The Mallards have brought their cousin. He's the most utter dud.'

'Good Lord, here come the gang from the Rectory! I never expected they'd turn up. There probably won't be enough to eat, or something awful.'

Yes; at the end of the short visit, her vision of married life with him had come into focus amazingly. It was almost real to her now.

The two of them stand together, in their tennis things, on the steps, full in the evening sunshine. The loaded runabout, three in the dickey, moves away. Cheerio. Thanks most fearfully. Come again soon. Good-bye. The court was a bit lumpy to-day, wasn't it? Did you notice how the services broke at the far end? I think I'll give it a roll now. There's time before dinner. Heavens, that's the third time we've forgotten to slack the net. You had bad luck in the singles. It's my own fault. My volleying is rotten.

What I like about the Pages is that they're such terrific *pals*, if you take what I mean —

Victor (roaring with laughter):

'She steals all my pullovers. And I haven't a tie to my name.'

Joan (roaring with laughter):

'When I'm hard up for pocket-money I win it off him at billiards. He's fearfully conceited about his play.'

'Don't you dance with my husband if you value your toes.'

'Don't you touch any of that cake. My wife made it.'

[When I am asked what good the War has done us, I say this: That it has brought about a cleaner, saner relationship between the sexes.

The young people of to-day, with their short-cut hair and simple healthy clothing are a whole world away from the days of Oscar collars and hobble-skirts. To see a couple of them together is to see something very like the jolly out-door sort of friendship of a pair of boys. There is none of the nasty old atmosphere of sexual innuendoes and concealments. Nowadays, there is no concealment, for the excellent reason that there is nothing to hide.]

One day, she had asked:

'Victor, we're going to have children, aren't we?'

'Oh, Lord, yes! I should rather think we are. Dozens.'

If only she were not so intensely aware of his *physical* presence. Sometimes, in a room, when she was not looking at him and he stood near her, she imagined that she could feel his exact position, his attitude. And this was humiliating, because he most certainly didn't have the same sensation, to anything like the same extent. Quite natural, of course. After all, I'm nothing to miss the Boat Race for, now; and when my complexion's gone I shall be a perfect hag. Whereas, Victor — well, Philip had cross-questioned the maid into admitting that she put him second. Not quite

up to Ramon Novarro. But above Ronald Cole-
man, and streets off poor Rudie.

Humiliating, sometimes, and disgusting. Not
so much for the family likeness to goats, bitches,
cats. That any sensible girl gets used to before
she's nineteen. But for the things which, every
now and then, seemed to jump out of her mouth
of their own accord. Things which she saw
afterwards were idiotic, vile. Pre-war. And she
had to defend them.

'Do you love me?'

He had pretended at first not to hear. She
repeated it.

First he looked surprised. Hullo, what's the
joke? Then merely red.

And she, because she felt she'd be physically
sick if one of them didn't say something, put on
a teasing schoolgirl's voice:

'Go on, do you or don't you? I want to know.'

'I don't in the least see – '

'Never mind. I want to hear you say it – '

Later, she had to ask:

'I annoyed you, just now, didn't I?'

'Not in the slightest.' He looked away.

'You thought I was silly, didn't you?'

'No – '

'Liar.'

'Well, if you insist on knowing: Yes.'

'That's right. I agree with you. But what I want to know is – what were you ahsamed of?'

'So far as I know, I'm not ashamed of anything. But I'm afraid I don't at all understand what you mean.'

Such were the mud-banks. But how ungenerous, captious, to shove on to them; when there is plenty of room in mid-stream and the water sparkles like Cambridge Backs; a bit shallow, but deep enough for a punt. And what could have been nicer than his behaviour to her in front of his other, older girl friends? Who were probably all jealous. I could have understood so-and-so; but where on earth did he dredge up *this?* Victor was never guilty even of the venial tactlessness of referring to things which had happened before Joan and he had met. If any of them did so, he practically snubbed them. And he remembered little things she liked. The crop with the darker handle. Bull's eyes. The deck-chair with arms.

. . . .

After her return from Wildlands, there were no more visits. But Victor would run up to Town in the car as often as three times a week;

sometimes taking them out to the country, sometimes spending the day at Bellingham Gardens. There was talk of a combined holiday up the river, a little later on.

Meanwhile, he was kept supplied with the latest family news. The news seemed chiefly to be Philip.

Things looked black at the office. Nearly every day, Philip would have something, quite impersonally, to report. He had forgotten to address some envelopes. He had filed two letters wrongly. Was he doing it on purpose? Not exactly. He had adopted that special attitude of fatalism which seems to make misfortunes descend like a shower-bath.

Victor began to enjoy a most awkward position. Everybody confided in him.

'Victor, darling, I've been so much looking forward to the opportunity of a really good talk with you. It's about Philip. . . . I sometimes feel that you really know and understand him much better than any of us.'

'Oh, I say, Mother – '

'But I mean that seriously, my dear. For one thing, you're a man. You, perhaps, can explain what, to a woman, seems unreasonable! I should tremendously like to be able to grasp Philip's point of view. Lately, he's been quite changed, as though he were a different person altogether. . . . I confess I'd never meant you to be troubled with any of this. I'd hoped it was a phase which would pass; and it seemed unfair to load you with our family worries. But lately, I've begun to feel – well, I won't say alarmed. . . .

'And then, there are other reasons. Of course, you know Allen Chalmers, don't you? Well, I don't wish for one moment, by this, to say a word against his personal character, you understand – but I do and shall maintain that he is *not* a good friend for Philip to have. I think he unsettles him, and puts all kinds of discontented ideas into his head. They meet regularly. . . .'

There was more of this. Victor asked, at length:

'Then, what, exactly, do you want me to do?'

'Oh, if you could just say something . . .'

She was vague. Her vagueness reminded him that he was more than half committed to the opposite party.

'I suppose,' he began tentatively, 'that this job of Philip's is an awfully good one, isn't it?'

'Oh, yes. It was got for him by an old friend of my late husband's. It isn't the sort of thing one could pick up anywhere. It's got the most excellent prospects.'

The words did not greatly impress him. Philip had been more vivid. He asked:

'But if Philip is getting into trouble about his work like this; surely he won't do much good at it?'

'Oh, I know . . . I know. . . .'

She was really quite helpless.

'It's all most dreadfully difficult. One doesn't know *where* to turn.'

'I know it's most important about the prospects, but the real question is, are you specially keen on Philip sticking to that particular job; or would you just as rather he took another, if that had got prospects, too? He seems to have such an objection to this one.'

'Well, of course, I had rather set my heart on Mr. Eliott's business. It was nice in so many ways. And I always felt it was the sort of thing my husband would have so approved of. . . . But, of course, if Philip wishes otherwise, I can say no more. I mustn't stand in his way. He must think of himself, not of me. . . .'

Victor began to fear tears. He continued hastily:

'You mean that if a job could be found for

189

Philip of a different kind but with prospects just as good, you'd allow him to leave this one?'

'Naturally, I would. . . . I should urge him to do so, as he seems so unhappy here. But I'm afraid,' Mrs. Lindsay wanly smiled, 'that that other job would be very difficult to find.'

'I'm afraid it would,' Victor agreed.

They did not seem to have got much further; but he prided himself that he had at least been diplomatic in Philip's cause, in getting his mother to admit the mere possibility of change. Mrs. Lindsay added:

'There's just one thing, Victor dear, about Allen Chalmers. l wouldn't, if I were you, mention the subject to Joan.'

'Why not?' He was startled.

'Well, I've done so already. And she simply won't hear a word against him. It's such a pity to make unpleasantness over a thing like that. Much better just to ignore it. The darling child's so generous towards everyone. Though I'm afraid, in this case, that her generosity is rather misplaced.'

He said nothing. Mrs. Lindsay did not see how deep her words had gone. None the less he resolved, at the first opportunity, to hear Joan's opinion of Chalmers from her own mouth.

That same day, she herself asked him:

'Victor, what *are* we to do for Philip?'

A little tired after her mother's harangue, he replied good-humouredly:

'It's Philip every time I come into this house.'

To his discomfiture, she flashed into anger:

'I'm sorry. I ought to have known our affairs would bore you, sooner or later.'

'Joan, I never meant anything of the kind – '

'I suppose Mother's been talking to you?'

'I should think she has. For the last hour. I've been trying to get her to make a regular statement of what she does want – '

The comic sincerity of this and his injured looks convinced her.

'I'm sorry. I beg your pardon. I seem to be developing the most awful temper.' She smiled. 'This house is full of sparks, just now.'

Victor left London that day with an oppressive sense of importance. They seemed all to be vaguely relying on him to do something. What – nobody quite knew. The problem grew less weighty as he drove away from it, scorching along the Portsmouth Road. He had to be back at Wildlands for dinner. An old friend of his uncle's was coming; just returned from Africa.

CHAPTER XIV

'My dear, I'm only trying to make you see how utterly fantastic the whole idea is. Why, it would kill him inside a year.'

Victor slightly shrugged his shoulders and began walking the hearthrug again.

'I suppose you're right.'

'Of course I'm right. How long have you known Phil? How long have I?'

'Oh, you've rubbed that in quite enough already, thanks. I'm perfectly aware I ought never to have interfered – ' his resentment showed once more – 'even when asked to.'

Joan, huddled up on the sofa, sighed:

'Don't be an idiot. I'm not blaming you. All I object to is your persistent idea that there's really something in the scheme, all the time.'

'Naturally I thought so at first. Otherwise, do you suppose I'd have suggested it?'

'But do you now?'

'Well, no, I suppose I don't. As you seem so positive that Philip isn't fit enough for the life. Personally, I should have thought that, after the first, it'd have done him good. When he got used to it.'

'But that's just what you can't understand,' she cried, almost in tears of impatience. 'There are things he'd never get used to. Oh, it's the whole way he's been brought up. I can't explain. Either you see it, or you don't – '

'I must say, Joan, I've sometimes thought you all make rather an extra invalid of him. Of course, I know he's delicate – '

'The fact is,' said Joan, with a pale, weary frown, 'it's no earthly good our discussing this. Oh, yes – I'm quite aware I started it.'

'But listen,' he continued hastily. 'I absolutely agree with you. You tell me the scheme's no use. You're his sister. That's enough for me.'

She did not change her listless attitude, staring in front of her. She spoke, as it were, half to herself:

'After all, whether we agree or not's beside the point. We can't do anything to stop him. He wouldn't listen to you or to me.'

'That's just what I can't get at. You talk about him as if he were a kid. But I suppose he'd got some reason for making up his mind. Nobody even advised him what to do. And he seemed to take to the notion from the very beginning. He wanted to settle it at once.'

'Yes, that's exactly it.' She roused herself again. 'Couldn't you see from his manner that there was something queer about it? And that look he gave Mother. Does one decide to go to the South Pole, just like that, in an evening; when you've scarcely left England before in your life?'

'There's a good deal of difference between Kenya and the South Pole. . . . And I don't see that he was in such a fearful hurry, considering. We talked it over for nearly two hours and he asked lots of questions. After all, there's not much time to waste.'

'I know. That's the awful thing about it. Phil will rush his head into this before he's got rid of the idea, or whatever it is, which is making him do it.'

'I must say, I don't see where all this appalling mystery comes in. You were there a few weeks ago, when we had that long discussion. Philip said he wanted fresh air, time to write, an outdoor job, and so forth. That was what I naturally remembered. It simply flashed on me; here's the chance! My uncle says it's practically hopeless trying to get that sort of job in England. And there were the prospects. Making him a partner in the plantation if he did well. You heard all that. I mean to say, the thing seemed as if it was going to fit like a glove. Surely, there's enough reasons for you. Philip's a sportsman. I'd have been rather surprised, myself, if he'd refused.'

She smiled wanly.

'Victor, we're wasting time.'

'Well, what do you want me to do?'

'You? Oh, nothing. . . . There's nothing you can do, is there?'

She was so preoccupied with her thoughts as to be unaware, for a moment, of the wounding suggestion in her words. She added:

'Oh, yes, there is, though. I want you to promise me, whatever Phil says, not to give a definite answer to your uncle's friend, or arrange for Phil to meet him, before Saturday. That's the latest day, isn't it? Well, I know Phil will try to settle this at once. Tell him it's impossible or something – see?'

'Just as you like.'

'And, Victor,' she was aware, now, of his deeply aggrieved manner, 'you do realize, don't you that whatever happens, I'm most awfully grateful to you for trying to help like this. I mean, your scheme might so easily have been something really possible, mightn't it?'

But he was still cold, and she was too heavy-hearted then to care for the trouble of more elaborately repairing their difference. She sighed, for a second time, and left the room.

She was going to see Allen.

'I'm afraid you're unlucky,' said the landlady. 'This is the one day in the week when Mr. Chalmers doesn't get back till seven.'

There was nothing to do but wait. She paced up and down his dingy room. Presently the landlady brought up a cup of cocoa.

'It'll help to pass the time, even if you don't want it much,' she explained.

At last they heard his footsteps on the stairs.

'What's wrong?' was his first question.

Then, when they were alone:

'I expect you'd rather talk in the street. The cooking's a bit strong, isn't it?'

She agreed. Movement suited her uneasy mood. They walked up and down, the whole length of the road, between the tall houses, whose gulf was already in the shadow. She began, rapidly, to describe what had happened. He listened, puffing at his huge pipe, glancing down sideways, every few moments, at her ring-finger. An imbecile boy, one of the neighbours, (most of whom had some such affliction in the family) was leaning out of a top storey window, high in the evening sunlight, foolishly waving the fragment of a mirror. Her opal sparked as the ray touched it.

'What's your mother's attitude?' he asked, presently.

'Oh, she's more or less neutral. At first, she didn't take it seriously. Now, I think, she's already beginning to realize that Phil's made up his mind. By degrees, she'll get alarmed. Meanwhile, she's saying what a splendid thing it'll be for Phil and how it'll make a new man of him. She doesn't seem to grasp that if he doesn't change his mind before next Saturday, he'll agree to go. And that, if he agrees, in less than a month he'll be gone. Oh' – Joan broke out suddenly, the tears in her eyes – 'I felt so furious with her at breakfast, this morning. Doesn't she know her own son? Hasn't she any imagination?'

'She's got too much,' said Allen, 'if she can see Philip on a coffee plantation.'

Joan felt some suspicion, however, of this last remark. She was quick to challenge it:

'But Mother's wrong there, too. Most of all. Of course Phil could do well at the job, if he set his mind to it. Mother thinks he'd just sit about and cry because he hadn't got his favourite cigarettes. People imagine he's namby and soft. That's just where they're so utterly wrong. If he gets an idea into his head he'll force himself to go through with it, by sheer will-power, until he

breaks down. It's his health isn't strong enough.
They can't understand how terribly dangerous
it is to goad him on like this. He'd do anything – '

Her absurd, half touching, half infuriating
faith in her brother. If she had asked him then,
direct: Do you agree with me? he would, out of
mere sympathy for her, have answered: No.

'Am I to see him to-night?'

'No. We can't do anything till to-morrow.
Victor's there.'

She had let slip the name. Worse, its context
seemed to imply a deceit or conspiracy against her
lover. She felt bound, immediately, to continue:

'You heard, of course.'

'Yes.' He added, with the quaint, rather stiff
politeness which occasionally reminded her of his
country rectory home:

'I ought to congratulate you.'

'I'd much rather you didn't,' she said, smiling.

They reached his door, for the ninth or tenth
time. Joan looked at her watch.

'Heavens! it's twenty-five to eight. I must rush
for dinner.'

'Have some with me?'

'It would be fun. . . . But I can't possibly.'

'I'm to come after eight o'clock to-morrow?'

'Yes. And Allen, you will do your best, won't you? If you fail, there's nobody. For goodness' sake, find out why Phil's so obstinate.'

He nodded, but would not promise. Feeling a slight impulse to watch her out of sight round the corner of the street, he turned, with characteristic perversity, and went indoors.

'Where *have* you been, darling?' Mrs Lindsay asked. 'We were getting quite alarmed.'

They had just finished their meal and were all still in the dining-room. The thought flashed through her mind – if I tell, Phil will guess that we've been planning something, and that'll make him more obstinate than ever. So she answered:

'Oh, round about the place, you know. I forgot to keep my eye on the clock.'

She looked at Victor and saw that he was not yet over his resentment. When she had hastily eaten something, she tried to get an opportunity of speaking to him alone. But it was late now, and he had soon to go home.

.   .   .   .

'And so it's more or less fixed?'

Allen lay back in his chair, careful to show neither too much nor too little astonishment.

'Utterly, as far as I'm concerned.'

'You've certainly wasted no time.'

'Why should I? One saw the chance and took it.'

Philip's manner, from the first moment, had been semi-aggressive. He looked liverish, a nasty sallow colour. He stood up or wandered about the room and kept fiddling with things. His eyes were evasive. Allen remarked, faintly smiling:

'Another of your lightning decisions.'

'You think it amusing?' Philip was on guard at once.

'Yes – I suppose I do.'

'You're right. It's ironic, somehow,' – this was a harsher, less balanced tone than Philip's usual voice of piqued impartiality, 'that I should be the one to do something at last, after all these years of talk. And that you, who, one felt, might any day commit a murder or join the Foreign Legion, remain stuck in your hospital, which you're always declaring you hate so much.'

'I'm afraid you flatter me,' Allen grinned. 'The truth is, you're avoiding my questions. You haven't so far produced a single adequate motive for all this. Only a lot of commonsense reasons, which are without the slightest importance and wouldn't, by themselves, make you so much as get out of bed in the morning. You never did anything commonsense in your life; and I refuse to believe that you're beginning now.'

'It's amazing how you love to dramatize everything.' But Philip's show of softening was only momentary. 'Well, for your benefit, we'll put it that this is my answer to a whole attitude which I've been aware of against me steadily for the last six months.'

Allen's eyebrows did not move.

'On the part of your mother?'

'Yes. And of others.'

One is seldom quite prepared for proofs of a resentment against one's self. Allen, who could take most things calmly, was betrayed into remarking:

'Well, let's hope the answer will be properly appreciated.'

Philip said nothing. There was a long stupid pause. Out of which Allen brought abruptly:

'Look here. This is all very fine. Have you the smallest conception of what you're doing?'

'I hope I'm not a total idiot.'

That Philip felt no surprise at the question might have seemed strange. Much more so was his not pretending to feel any.

'Does it mean anything more to you to go to East Africa than to take an excursion to Southend? I'll tell you. It means less.' Allen sat up in his chair. 'Philip, your imagination wants lancing. It's swollen with pus.'

Philip made a slight movement, fastidious, of annoyance and distaste.

'Here we are in Kensington, with our cigarettes and our talk. We make our little hits and gestures. We're intellectually justified. Oh, yes. Occasionally, even, our position is morally sound. But have you thought what satisfaction there is in being justified in a quarrel with people you're several thousand miles away from? When I was seven, I used to say: I wish the castor oil would make me die. Then Nannie'll be a murderess. . . . Without wishing to be offensive, I must say I think you overrate you mother's sensibilities if you imagine that, after a few tears dripped into the dock, you won't just become a cipher: My boy in Kenya. We're all so proud of him. Talk about cutting off one's nose – Haven't you, well, even enough sense of humour to see that?'

'Need we discuss this?' said Philip.

.   .   .   .

Allen met Joan in the hall.
'I'm sorry,' he told her.
'But, Allen; what are we to do?'

'Let him go, I suppose.'

'Unless he changes his mind at the last moment.'

He did not reply.

'But, Allen, you will come again, won't you? Have one more try.'

'If you think it's worth while, send me a line,' he said.

She saw that he did not. For a moment, even, she was angry with him. 'He doesn't care,' she thought. 'Nobody cares.'

.   .   .   .

Thus arrived Saturday, and, in the evening, Philip went to dine with Colonel Page to meet Mr. Wells, the coffee planter, at his club. Victor, at the last minute, was unable to join them.

Mr. Wells was thinner than his friend, and very nervous in his movements. He looked devoured by the sun. He talked with a kind of hungry heartiness, in the voice of an Army chaplain. There appeared to be no question whatever as to whether Philip would be engaged. He was greeted as though the matter had been settled beforehand.

During dinner, the older men talked to each other, barely admitting him into the conversation, even by courtesy. But afterwards, Mr. Wells, cigar in hand, began to deliver a sort of lecture, smiling into vacancy before him:

'It's the most wonderful country in the world,' he said.

'My place is just two hundred and fifty acres. I run it with my pal. Very decent sort. Old Hockey Blue. But he doesn't want to stay out there after next year. The more fool he, I tell him.

'Great difficulty is native labour. Natives don't make good neaparas – headmen, in the lingo. Want watching. We're teaching 'em Soccer.

'Hard work, some of it. But the temperature's nothing to grouse at. Five thousand odd feet up. And after five, we're free for games.

'People talk about the wilds. No more wilds than Surrey. Kyambu. Kikuyu district. We drop into Nairobi once a month. Theatres. Dances. Cup Final. Kenya Derby. Just like Town.

'But London's a cold-shouldered sort of hole. Our social life's one long hum. We have people dropping in every day. Usually someone staying in the house. Tennis whenever we've a few minutes to spare. And cricket.

'Polo's the latest craze. Everyone turns out. We've all got something to ride. And I can tell you we get some very sporting chukkas. Fellow smashed his collar bone just before I came away.

'I think the real beauty of the place is that it's like one big family. We all know all about each other. All our little faults and fads. Everything. And we just make the whole thing into a huge joke. That's why the life's got such tremendous go.'

When Philip went home that night, all was settled. He felt as though he had been sitting, throughout the evening, in front of an enormous, blazing fire; which had, nevertheless, the strange property of making one feel gradually more and more freezingly cold.

CHAPTER XV

CURRANTS bought a map of Equatorial Africa. 'Do you know,' she confessed, 'I couldn't even have told you whicn coast Philip was going to be nearest to?'

She also remarked:

'We shall have to drink lots and lots of coffee, now.'

Mrs. Lindsay and she had both wept when they heard the news of the decision.

'Darling, I do so hope you'll be happy. It'll be dreadful for us to have to part with you. But I know it's for your own good. We must try to remember that.'

The two women spent all their time in making things. A housewife. A new jumper, (the nights are chilly). A case for handkerchiefs. A blotting-book, with pockets for envelopes and papers.

The doctor examined Philip, and pronounced him quite fitted for the climatic conditions, which are in no way severe.

This was Joan's last hope. She would not allow herself to believe that he was right. But what difference did that make?

She was now frankly wretched.

'Phil, I simply can't believe that you honestly want to go.'

The only thing possible was that they should quarrel.

'If you knew how I'm dying to get out of this house.'

'You mean, you want to leave us so much?'

He had answered impatiently:

'Oh, you belong to Victor now.'

'Phil – ' the very suspicion horrified her, 'it isn't because of that – ?'

'My dear girl, of course not.'

'If I thought it was,' she was serious, 'I believe I'd give him up.'

For a moment, he was moved. But only for a moment. Affection, in his present state, repelled him. He feared its power.

'For God's sake,' he said, 'don't be so theatrical. You talk as if I was on the steps of the scaffold.'

He forced his tone down to the pitch of reason, matter-of-fact:

'You must see that, as things are at present, I can't stay at home any longer. It's really essential that I don't see mother for a bit.'

'A bit!' she laughed sadly. 'How many years does that mean?'

'Oh, Joan, I know it's not nice going away for a long time. It never is. But I'm certain that this scheme is the best thing I could do. I may seem a bit depressed now, but that doesn't mean I'd change anything that's going to happen. Yes, I've thought it all over; you needn't worry about that. You know, I've always said I wanted to get away from London.'

'I suppose so,' she answered, listlessly. Her look into his face was questioning. He saw, with a sinking of the heart, that he had half-convinced her.

Philip had already given up his work at the office. There was nothing for him to do at Bellingham Gardens. Few enough preparations had to be made for the journey. One or two people wished to say good-bye to him. And there were some clothes to get.

He read novels, shut up in his sitting-room, all the mornings and afternoons. He was drowsy and heavy-headed. He had no longer any fears of a nervous breakdown. The three weeks' sea voyage to Kilindini would put him right again.

He had strongly supported the plan that Victor should spend the last week before the voyage at Bellingham Gardens.

He became eager for cinemas, theatres. The women, delighted to have found so simple a means of pleasing him, came with him nearly every night.

They scarcely spent an evening at home. Currants said:

'We shall remember this all our lives, shan't we?'

Occasionally, he surprised between them some reference to an event which would take place after he had left England. This was like the stripping of his bed on the morning of his leaving for the preparatory school. His mother had never had the tact to postpone it.

He was losing all violent feeling towards her now. She cried a little and was affectionate, but she lacked significance. The idea of a revenge seemed anachronized, tasteless as an ice wafer. Once or twice, he had said something brutal:

'Well, thank God – all this isn't for much longer.'

She shed a few helpless tears. It was like tormenting an animal. Meaningless.

.   .   .   .

Allen received a note from Joan. She begged him to make another effort.

He went the same evening, without having in the least made up his mind what it would be best to say. 'Certainly,' he thought, 'if Philip changes his mind now, he'll never admit it to me. Probably it's too late for him to change it at all.

Joan's being extraordinarily dense, chivvying him
like this.'

'Mr. Philip told me he was out to everyone,
sir.'

'Just tell him it's me, will you, please?'

The maid soon returned:

'Mr. Philip says he's sorry but he's very busy.
He'll send you a line to say good-bye.'

Allen, more amused than angry, turned to go
down the steps. He had not heard the car draw up.
Victor and he passed each other within an inch,
face to face. Neither spoke.

.   .   .   .

Victor, come to spend the night, had arrived
sooner than he had intended. Joan found him
in the sitting-room, talking to her mother.

As soon as they were alone, he brought out,
very red:

'There's something I want – I've been wanting,
to mention to you, Joan. I hadn't meant to do
it . . . only, just as I came in now, I met Allen
Chalmers. He'd been to see Philip.'

'Yes. I sent for him.'

'You sent for him? But why on earth. . .'

'To try and argue with Phil – oh, don't let's
discuss it. I'd rather not.'

'I think it ought to be discussed.'

She looked at him; taking in, with half-impudent anger, the schoolboy gravity which he must have worn as a house prefect.

'And why?'

'You know quite well.'

'Oh, I understand,' she flashed, after an instant's pause, 'Mother's been talking to you. No doubt she's told you all about the other time Allen came to the house; after I'd been to see him. And about the lie I made up. . . Though I don't quite follow how she found it out.'

He was dazed:

'The lie. . . ? Mother hasn't told me a word.'

'Well, I *did* tell one. And I have asked Allen *twice* to come here. Now. What do you think of that?'

Victor, scarcely audible, pronounced a sentence ending:

' . . . suppose it's none of my business.'

'If it's none of your business, then I don't see what right you've got to insinuate things about Allen. You know absolutely nothing against him.'

At this he was defiant again:

'As a matter of fact, I do.'

'What is it?' He was silent. 'Go on. You've got to tell me now.'

'I don't see why – '

'Tell me.'

Crimson, he muttered something garbled:

'When I first met Philip at the hotel. . .'

'Good gracious, is that all?'

She burst into rather exaggerated laughter.

'All – ?'

'Yes. I've known that for months.'

'Who told you – ?' He managed to ask.

'Allen did, himself. And Victor, I must say, I think you're very narrow-minded. As if a thing like that mattered.'

He left the room.

.   .   .   .

Dinner that evening was not so bright as usual. Victor was inclined to be sullen, and Joan scarcely spoke. Indeed it was Philip who revived their spirits.

'When are you coming out to join me?' he asked.

'When we're married.' Victor grinned.

The word startled her. During these three weeks, she had barely given their engagement a thought.

'Oh, I shall be home by that time. A million-aire.'

Currants smiled. And Victor, perhaps with design, asked:

'How much will you take to let me have the job? I'm getting jealous.'

'Not for sale, I'm afraid.'

Philip laughed. The sound made Joan almost shudder.

.   .   .   .

One big family.

In the station brake, the boy with a glass eye had given him a horse-bite, asked his name and then lost interest. They were asking the clergyman-master who he thought would be new caps. Three loud groans as they passed the Olde Tea Shoppe and the Royal Beacon Hotel. Three hisses as they turned into the drive. Glad to be back. Please, sir, I want to go home. Let's rebel. We're going to chuck you out into that gorse-bush, sir. Oh, sir, you're hurting.

The front porch, with that iron-work hanging lamp. A maid looking down from one of the dormitory windows. Rawson, show that new boy his peg and locker, and then bring him in to tea. Come on. A baize notice board in the passage. The following will be week-captains. Any boy found ragging or fooling in the lavatories will be severely dealt with.

The dining-room smelt of bread. Damp crumbs.

Philip lay yawning, shivering. It must have turned much colder. He felt for his watch on the table beside his bed. Nearly three. He ought to get some sleep, somehow. The aspirins were in Joan's room.

For the first day or two, the new boys hung about the passages, keeping together. Garvel got lammed for using a Senior's bat. Bennet was the one who didn't understand the rule about wearing nailed shoes in the gym. They talked and quarrelled among themselves. Alsop said: 'I'll take on anyone at Ju-Jitsu.' On Sundays, they had to write home. Mr. Driutt chalked up bits of news as suggestions on the blackboard. We beat Hilldown by an innings.

My darling Mother,

I am quite certain that I shall always loathe and detest this place. Do please come and take me away as soon as you possibly can. I *hate* it.

214

On Wednesday and Saturday mornings he had woken feeling pains in his bowels. These were half holidays; and, after tea, Mr. James would come down and give the Lower Game fielding practice.

Philip sat up, turned on the light and smoked a cigarette. He felt calmer, and was presently asleep.

In the dream, he saw the coaches of a train. The train had just stopped. It was alongside a long, low continental platform, and the carriage doors were breast-high with his line of vision. It was raining. Several people stood and watched.

He realized that he was not really on the platform, but inside the coach. The people were waiting for him to come out of it. The train would not move. The engine had been uncoupled. A most dreadful terror seized him. They waited. Nothing happened.

All the time, a reasonable voice, kept arguing with, persuading him. There's nothing whatever to be alarmed about. Can't you understand? I promise you; you're among friends.

Philip woke, perspiring. The electric light was still on. He got out of bed, and, raising the window blind a little, saw the dawn of his final day at Bellingham Gardens, in a mountainous and chilly sky, above roofs already cold with rain.

.   .   .   .

It had been arranged that Victor should take them out into the country in the car. They were to return in time for a theatre, that evening. But the drizzle which was falling steadily during breakfast made the idea of a long drive under the hood uninviting. They decided against it.

There seemed nothing to do. Mrs. Lindsay fussed over last little details of packing. Lunch came, after hours. The afternoon had a hollow sound, as though the house were empty. It began to grow strangely dark. The hall sank into an evening gloom. The stained-glass fanlight, shedding its colours feebly on brown shadow, gave to the place something of the ugliness of a chapel.

Joan went to the sitting-room window:
'Oh, look,' she exclaimed suddenly. 'Look.'
'What's up?' said Victor, coming to her side.
'At this time of year . . . isn't it weird?'
'Nothing's weird in this rotten climate.'
But Joan felt really dismayed – frightened

almost – by the extraordinary happenings out of doors. For slowly, along the pavement, under the ragged trees, there was oozing a fog, a thick 'pea-soup' fog, which writhed in strong spirals against the house-fronts, building itself up, layer upon layer, like coil upon coil of inch-thick cable, until it reached the tiles; then sinking upon itself, then rising again, voluminously, an enormous stack of vapour, like cotton-wool which had been soaked in oil.

'I don't know how we shall manage the theatre, if it goes on like this,' said Currants.

'Oh, that'll be all right,' Victor reassured her. 'If the worst comes to the worst we can get to the underground station, somehow.'

'In that case, we'd better dress early; so as to start in good time.'

They stood about. Then, at Mrs. Lindsay's suggestion, played Old Maid. To Joan, the false-ness of the pastime was scarcely tolerable. In her present condition, heightened by the sinister aspect of the weather, and miserably unlike her usual self, it would have been a relief to her had they openly discussed East Africa all day long. Philip seemed to her even unusually controlled. Her mother had made her consciousness of the occasion visible in every gesture. Currants, incapable of more than one emotion at a time, was enjoying herself, as sincerely as she would be crying to-morrow. As for Victor, she was inclined now to think him tactfully cheerful, now callous. She could not judge.

At last, they had to go upstairs. They did so all together. A few moments later, Joan, opening her door, saw Philip crossing the landing. Such was the state of her nerves that she actually started a little.

'I'm just going to get my shoes. I must have left them downstairs,' he said.

Twenty minutes later, she was dressed. Victor joined her in the sitting-room.

'Let's go down and talk to Philip,' he suggested.

His tone pleased her.

'Of course we will. I didn't know he was ready yet.'

'Yes. He must be. I looked into his bedroom as soon as I was. He wasn't there, then.'

It was difficult, later, to be sure whether, at some faintest premonition, she had not hurried down the basement stairs. Philip's door was wide open. A scrap of paper lay conspicuously on the bare table.

At any rate, now, on the threshold, she stopped

dead; so suddenly that Victor, close behind, nearly pushed her forward into the room. With a small gasp of apology, he halted; confronted the surprise:

'Why, there's no one here.'

CHAPTER XVI

An hour later there was a wind. The fog was fanned westward, up into the air. Inflated volumes of it drifted down the street, slowly rising. The rain-gusts followed, obliquely driven, skidding along the pavement.

Victor closed the sitting-room door gently behind him. She turned, dazed, from the glass and saw his outline murky within the shadow. The daylight was feeble already.

'Mother's better now,' he said. 'Miss Durrant's with her.'

He was pale. One could see still how much he had been scared.

'She won't hear of the doctor. But I wish we could get a sleeping-draught. Would the chemist be able to recommend something safe, do you think?'

'He'll be shut now.'

Joan sat down in the nearest chair. She yawned with wretchedness.

'Isn't there a door where you can get medicine?'

'Yes, I believe so.'

The drops squeaked on the pane. The little silver clock raced on into Time, like a horse with the post in sight.

'You'd better have something to eat.'

'I couldn't.'

'You must. You can't do without.'

'You have something.'

'Not unless you do.'

He was worried, anxious to help them all. She felt as though she had been skinned. Trembling for the first touch on the raw.

'Joan, you must. What'll they think downstairs if we don't?'

'They can think what they like.'

He hesitated:

'I've just said to the maid, quite casually, of course, that Philip's been called away suddenly on business and that he mayn't be back for several days.'

'I don't see what good that can do.'

'Do you think,' he was patient, 'I ought to have told her what's happened?'

'Of course.'

'But supposing Philip does come home?'

'Is that likely?' She was scornful.

'It think it's quite possible.'

'What do you imagine his note meant?'

'Oh, well – he wrote that in a hurry, didn't he?'

'Of course he wrote it in a hurry. He barely had time to write it at all.'

'That isn't quite what I'm driving at. Don't you think that perhaps — you know, it often happens — he may have lost his memory or, well — something of that kind, just for a few hours?'

She ought never to have allowed him to come and talk to her. She ought to have locked herself up in her bedroom; she was unfit for any kind of decent behaviour. Mother had let off *her* steam. Ugh!

'Don't be idiotic.'

It was like kicking one's spaniel. He said:

'Let me bring you something to eat, in here.'

'Poor Victor, you're hungry, naturally. And you won't admit it.'

'Never mind about me.'

Joan sat up, regarding him with hostile amusement.

'We've disgusted you, haven't we?'

He flushed.

'I don't — '

'Victor,' she cried, 'if you say that, I shall shake you! Can't you answer a question? What did you think of us, just now? What did you think of the way I spoke to Mother; wasn't that shocking?'

'It's no business of mine how you spoke to Mother,' he replied, with stiff distaste.

'No, I know that. But I'm asking what you

thought. And for heaven's sake don't talk like a boy in a Sunday school.'

His lips tightened obstinately. He said nothing.

She flung out, in a kind of despair:

'You're above us, aren't you? You're too good for us. Oh, I'm not sarcastic – '

He looked mistrustful, frightened.

'Do you know why I spoke to mother like that? Because I meant every word I said; and ought to have said a lot more. If it hadn't been for Mother, Philip'd never have left this house.'

'I don't see how you make that out,' he was moved to protest.

'Oh, I see it now, as plain as daylight. . . It was only her sneering made him so determined to take this loathsome Kenya job.'

'You haven't the smallest proof of that, you know. . . Philip was saying, right up to to-day how keen he was on it.'

'Well, why do you imagine he left?'

He had his motives for evasiveness.

'How should I know – ?'

'Tell me.' Again she was amused and hostile. 'You still defend Phil, do you? He's not disgraced himself in your eyes by running away?'

'I'm sure there was some good reason for it,' he answered, carefully.

'He ought to be honoured that you've got such faith in him.'

She mocked, hating herself. She was making herself hateful. It was no fault of his that he didn't know how to deal with her. Or didn't he chose to know? He was looking at her coldly. No wonder.

'I've changed my mind,' she said, suddenly, in a different, nervous voice; as though he might refuse her, 'would you ask Annie to bring some soup up on a tray to my room? Tell her I've got a headache.'

.   .   .   .

Victor met Currants on the landing.

'How is Mother now?'

'Oh, she's asleep.'

'I'm glad of that. I expect she'll be ever so much better when she wakes up. . . . By the way, I've been meaning to ask you, can you tell me the name of the street where Allen Chalmers lives?'

She did not know, off-hand. But there was an address-book in a drawer in the hall cupboard, where Allen, in far ago days when he was a stranger and more welcome guest, had written his.

'It's — ' Victor was confused, 'it's for something quite unimportant. I mean, there's no need to bother Mother or — anybody, by telling them.'

'Oh, no. Of course not.'

She agreed dully. She looked vague and lost. Her face was swollen with crying, as though she had been stung under the eyes by bees. Hastily pulling on a mackintosh, he strode out of the house.

.   .   .   .

'Take a chair,' said Allen, blandly.

'I can stand, thanks. I shan't keep you. I've come to know if you can tell me where Philip is.'

'What? Has he got lost on the way to Africa?'

Allen put his pipe on the mantelpiece and leaned against it. The room was quiet. The thick drawn curtains dulled the noise of the rain. A cone of lamplight illuminated their two heads, regarding each other above the table whose cloth was bordered with woollen pompoms.

'He cleared out of the house without any warning, about three hours ago.'

'Really? I haven't seen him.'

'Oh.'

There was a long pause. Victor did not move.

'Was that all you wanted to know?'

'Yes.'

'Well, I've told you – I haven't seen him.'

Another pause.

'Don't you believe me?'

'I'm afraid I don't, altogether.'

'That's unfortunate.'

Allen smiled. Victor was grim.

'It is, isn't it?'

A lorry rumbled slowly past outside, shaking the house.

'What are you going to do?'

'Search your rooms. And then ask your land-lady.'

Their voices held evenly to the pitch of conversation. No, there was a just audible falseness of tone. The negligence, the infinitesimal, apprehensive slurring of syllables, the slight deadening of the utterance, which one connects so intimately with: Well, what about it, then? Shall we, now? Right you are. I'm ready.

'My bedroom's on the next floor. The door facing you. Better take a candle. There's one here.'

Victor took it, without a word. Allen, his pipe in his mouth again, listened to the footsteps ascending, descending. He called:

'Mrs. Rose.'

'Yes, Mr. Chalmers?'

She appeared. Allen asked:

'This gentleman thinks somebody must have

called here to-day to see me, since tea-time. Did anyone come while I was out?'

'Oh, no, Mr. Chalmers. You know I always – '

'Yes, I know you do. That's why I felt sure they couldn't have. And certainly nobody's called since I've been home – ?'

'Oh, no – '

'Thank you.'

When she was gone, Allen put his pipe back on the mantelpiece. He asked, in his rather gentle voice:

'You heard?'

'Yes, I heard.'

'I suppose you'll have to apologise to me.'

'I shan't do anything of the kind. I'm pretty sure you know where Philip is. And I'm dead certain you persuaded him to leave home.'

'Well, you're wrong three times. Is there anything else?'

'Yes, this. I advise you not to show yourself at Bellingham Gardens any more.'

'Really. Why not?'

'You might find it unpleasant.'

'Whose message is that?'

'Everybody's.'

'It's your own, isn't it?'

'You'd better remember it, anyway.'

Victor turned, as if to go.

'Just one minute,' said Allen.

Victor staggered; took a large pace back. The lamp shivered and its flame gave a flutter. Allen half smiled. Down they went, rolling, mackintosh and all, missing the fender by inches. Gasping in each other's faces. Locked. At the second tap on the door, they broke loose.

'Come in.'

They had scrambled to their feet.

'I thought you might be glad of a warm-up before you go out into the wet,' said Mrs. Rose to Victor, smiling over her tray.

But he, muttering something, picked up his hat from the table and was gone.

'My friend's in a great hurry, I'm afraid.' Allen grinned. 'He was getting ready to go just as you came in.'

Allen drank both cups of cocoa, and wondered what had happened to Philip. Victor's call had lasted scarcely twenty minutes. 'He'd probably have killed me,' thought Allen, smiling. 'Mrs. Rose saved my life.'

CHAPTER XVII

I AM going away. It is not the least use trying to find out where.

A pulse in Philip's throat throbbed so hard that, at the top of the basement stairs, he stood still. His hat was on a chair in the hall. Nearly a minute passed. He turned the knob of the lock slowly, keeping his toe against the door to prevent its jarring. The paint inside the jamb, sticky even after months, made a noise like the opening of an envelope. He paused again, listening. A draught, through the narrow crack, stirred the tubular gong to a faint premonitory chime. Hastily, he let himself out into the fog.

He had been running for many minutes when he stopped to draw breath. Turning to the right from the gate, he had followed Bellingham Gardens along its continuation beyond the intersecting thoroughfare, north-eastward. Now he was within a crescent of mid-Victorian buildings; stately, decayed lodging-houses on the edge of the slum district. The fog wreathed itself about him. At moments, he could see up to the crooked wireless masts on the roofs. The traffic sounded loud yet indistinct. Car-hootings came only from behind; ahead was silence. His eyes were smarting. He shivered and became aware that he had forgotten his overcoat.

Philip put his hand to his breast pocket and drew out his leather wallet. The edges of the notes were all he wanted to see. Thirty-five pounds. His post office savings money, drawn a few days before, ready for the voyage. His bank account was being transferred direct to Nairobi.

Something brushed against his trouser-leg, making him start. It was only a cat. If he went back to the house now, at once, they wouldn't have missed him. Or he could say he had been out to post a letter. But there was the note, lying at this moment on the table in his room. Oh, he could find a dozen explanations –

Philip turned, and walked several paces towards his home. The traffic, by some trick of his imagination, now seemed fainter. When he paused again, it was to glance over his shoulders. The cat had utterly disappeared.

A man, who had been knocking at the doors of several houses, now came down from a flight of steps opposite and crossed the road with a bundle of papers in his hand.

'Lost yer wy, guv'nor?'

'Oh, no, thanks,' said Philip.

'Jest takin' a stroll like; for yer 'elth?'

Philip smiled and nodded. The man began talking, in clipped persuasive Cockney. He wanted to sell one of the printed sheets. It was a poem, written on behalf of ex-service men unemployed.

'I dunno where I shall sleep ter-night, and that's stryte.'

Philip had nothing less in his pocket than half-a-crown. He gave it; being rather rather afraid of the man, who was unshaven and wore a patched coat. The seller of poems was working westward. Philip again turned east.

A little way, and he met the cat. It mewed loudly, showing its teeth like a tiger. Philip sat down on somebody's front wall and regarded it. He felt that he had never looked at a cat before. It got into his lap with a bound. It was thin, and had a sore behind its ear. Its claw pricked Philip's thigh. He pushed it off and stood up. His teeth were chattering, though he did not feel cold. And he had a headache. He started off, briskly.

The fog was thinning. It was full of pockets and chasms. Then it began to blow past him in dirty shreds. He walked on more quickly; hurrying, running. He had not lost his way, but he had struck too far north. The rain began.

Philip turned up his coat collar and stood for some minutes in the archway of a court. The place was full of children, swarming about in the gloom, dodging each other, falling over; uttering weird shrieks, like seagulls in a cave. Errand boys, standing astride their bicycles, jeered at stout, prematurely developed girls in coats with cheap fur collars. Their imitation silk calves showed whitely; the heel screwing, as if unconscious. The rain wasn't going to stop.

A first objective appeared. He must have a mackintosh, and quickly. It was long past seven by now; the shops in the West End would be shut. Even here, within the darkening network of the slums, light gleamed only from the windows of small tobacconists, sweet-sellers. A curiosity shop and a saddler's were open late. The rain was coming down hard. He began to run in earnest, pausing merely for a hasty glance down side streets and alleys; bumping into people and getting cursed.

The pawnshop was not a big one. Its proprietor was just putting up the shutters. He led the way into a crowded, polymorphous interior, turned from behind the counter and briskly enquired:

'How much do you want for it, sir?'

Philip realized that he was holding his leather wallet in his hand. He had pulled it out, with a vague urgency, as soon as he had caught sight of the three golden balls. Still panting, he explained.

By the strangest coincidence, they hadn't a mackintosh. If he had come last week — But, still, there happened, luckily, to be just the thing. It was a dark, cumbrous-looking overcoat. Philip tried it on in the dim gaslight. It was on the large side. The sleeves had to be turned back; but, as the young Jew brightly explained, they could so easily be shortened. And it was worth three times the money. Fourteen shillings.

'It suits you very well, I think.'

Philip liked him. He paid and went out.

The overcoat was immensely thick. It made him feel how clammy his clothes were. If he had something to eat, it'd warm him up. Thank goodness, it wasn't too late for a meal. He would get down into Piccadilly, where there was some life. A few minutes' walk brought him to a main road and a 'bus.

The restaurant was crammed. White and gold, dazzling electricity, carpeted grape-crimson. At his table, a couple of flash young dagoes, in their Oxfords and high-cut waistcoats, were eating mash on toast and iced cakes. Philip ordered mash, too; and added a poached egg, tea and buns. He stuffed himself stupid.

The light made his head throb like a piston. He caught sight of himself in a wall-mirror. The overcoat was not so dark after all. It was dung-coloured, with large reddish-brown squares. The collar was astrakhan.

He tried to read the poem. It appealed directly, naïvely; from the ex-soldier to the civilian. We have nothing. You have everything. The electric lights blazed. Women with green hats. Men with rings. Sweating as they munched. The band blared triumph. Theirs. Anthropoid. Survival of the Unfittest.

When Philip got out into the street, he felt sick and his knees were trembling. The next hour was confused. Along the narrow streets running down towards the Embankment on either side of Charing Cross Station, he wandered, hunting for shelter, trying indiscriminately 'family,' 'commercial,' and 'private.' They were full up, or frankly distrusted him – unattended and without luggage. The rain kept on. The overcoat was his last moral support. As it grew wetter, it stank richly of what Philip vaguely identified as horse medicine. It was like an unfamiliar but reassuring companion. He turned up the astra-khan against his cheeks, right under his dripping hat.

A fat woman, with a prospect of gas-lit hall and staircase behind her, eyed his bedraggled figure coldly, but admitted that she had a bed to spare. She called shrilly for a consumptive-looking manservant whom Philip followed thank-fully up flights of rickety stairs to a bedroom, a tiny garret under the roof. The fat woman, who had bolted the front door, mounted after them. She was crudely and absurdly made up with rouge, eyebrow pencil and lip-stick. Her pink silk blouse reeked of mixed perspiration and cheap scent. She disliked Philip's appearance and showed it plainly, but her expression softened when he readily agreed to pay in advance.

He lay down on the bed wihout removing anything more than his coat and shoes. One glance at the stained damp-smelling sheets had resolved him not to undress. The attic had a damp, sour, heavy smell which filled his mind with curious and obscene associations. The window would not open more than a few inches. He lay down again and noticed that the plaster beside the bed was scribbled with drawings and lewd verses. One referred to the bell, which the

proprietress had once or twice reminded him
that he must ring if he wanted anything. A peal
of indistinct laughter was audible from below
stairs.

All at once, he began thinking, planning. His
head was dizzy with plans. He would go down
to Sussex to-morrow, to some quiet cheap village
inn, where he could live for weeks on his money.
Or would France be better? Once the fare was
paid. What about passports? Did they ask many
questions? Would they advertise for him, at
home? Or tell the police? Perhaps, after to-night,
the ports would be watched.

His temperature seemed to be undergoing
rapid changes. Sometimes his whole body was
shivering, sometimes perspiring. Glancing pains
shot over it, teasing the joints. His head ached
like a slow fire. It occurred to him that he was
about to have another attack of rheumatic fever.
'I shall die here,' he thought. 'They will not be
able to move me from this room.'

He lay cramped with terror as the hours of
the night almost interminably passed. His heart
was fluttering like a moth, sometimes missing a
beat. Rainy daylight advanced, in stages more
exquisitely prolonged than the moments of an
operation without anæsthetics. Before it came,

his self-control had broken down utterly. He uttered dry sobs. A little after three o'clock, he began to pray.

·   ·   ·   ·   ·   ·

Leaving the hotel early, after a breakfast which he was too sick to eat, he wandered along the Embankment. Smoke rolled up sullenly from the Surrey shore and hung in lowering wisps over the iron-dark water. A pleasure-steamer passed, bound for Hampton Court. The river ran swiftly against the breeze, which flicked the current into tiny heads of foam. Even if he had the nerve, they'd be in after him before he'd sunk twice. Selfridge's roof-garden was the place. Up on to the parapet and it's over. No, there's always the instant to consider when you feel your balance gone and see the pavement and the tops of the cars, and people's hats.

He looked up at Big Ben for the time. The clock-face was convex, concave. The light withered, went green. Total eclipse. People were bending above him. All talking.

'Where does he live?' asked someone.

'Where do you live?' a man shouted in his ear.

He gave the address. Mechanically, for he

237

was unable to add: Don't shout like that. I'm not deaf. He fainted again, and, recovering a little, was sick.

This made the small crowd draw back. But a clergyman, who happened to be passing, settled things with the police constable and volunteered to take the unfortunate young man home in a cab.

'Looks like one of the Reds,' a spectator murmured.

The astrakhan collar was quite ruined.

CHAPTER XVIII

Down the Boulevard he came, punctual, with his uncle's stride, between the lopped trees which had, in that cold March, not yet begun to sprout; knob-headed, resembling bags of golf-clubs.

Mrs. Lindsay opened the door:

'Dearest Victor, it is nice to see you again. . . . Joan, Victor's here! Oh, I expect she's with Philip. He's painting her, you know.'

'How is he?' Victor gravely asked, without comment.

'Oh, ever so much better, of course. This week we've been rather worried. He'd had a little cold. One has to be so tremendously careful.'

They went into the sitting-room. And there was Currants.

'Well; have you had a simply glorious term?'

Tea was all ready. He told them as much college news as his wandering attention could recall. It was extraordinary how much the place depressed his spirits, that afternoon. Extraordinary; because its appearance was unusually gay. The cretonnes had been washed. And when he had been there last, it was still a sick-house.

'So you only came down from Cambridge this

239

morning. We can never say you neglect us, can we?'

Scarcely noticing it, he was vaguely aware that Mrs. Lindsay had also changed. She was radiant. She looked years younger. She no longer seemed slightly timid, slightly apprehensive of something unpleasant about to happen. She was confidently gay.

He grinned perfunctorily.

She began referring to Philip's artistic successes, about which she was surprised to find that Joan had barely told him anything in her letters. 'Yes, last month, some friends of ours, Miss Oliver and Mrs. Clive – I believe you once met them here, didn't you? – had a stall at a bazaar in the Town Hall. It was a very grand affair. Opened by Lady – I forget her name, but she's the wife of an M.P. one often sees mentioned in the papers. And so, of course, they were tremendously anxious to get something quite out of the ordinary as their special *piece de résistance*. And they knew Philip painted. Well, we coaxed him to let us have three of his watercolours. Of course, he immediately said Mrs. Clive had chosen the worst of them all. But she had the best taste, in the end, it seemed; because, do you know, they fetched three guineas each? And two of them were sold on the first day!'

Victor had to rouse himself to an expression of astonishment.

'But you did hear, at any rate, of the great triumph?'

'No – er – I don't think so.'

'Oh, surely? Not about the poem? It's Mary's story, really.'

'Oh, no, Dorothy. You tell it.'

'Well, about six weeks ago, when Philip was over his second relapse, Mary gave us all such a wonderful surprise. She'd never told us anything about it beforehand, but she'd seen in some newspaper a competition for – what was it, Mary; the best Poem?'

'The Best Modern Poem.' Currants beamed and blushed.

'Yes, the Best Modern Poem. . . So, as it happened, just then, there'd been a regular tidy-up and turn-out of Philip's sitting-room. And Mary had picked up a poem of his which she'd found lying behind that old box where he keeps the gramophone records. It was about seagulls, wasn't it? . . . And then the idea came to her, and she made a copy of it, and sent it up to this paper. All on her own account. . . .

'And, do you know — the first prize was ten pounds. And, after three weeks, a letter came to say that Philip had won the second. Five. Wasn't it *good?* . . . Of course, we were all delighted. And the doctor said it had saved him a week of his convalescence.'

Victor agreed dully that it was wonderful.

'And, since then, we've had lots of excitements. Everybody's been so kind. Mr. Langbridge — you've often heard us talking about him, haven't you? — had a friend who's a journalist; and he's said that, when Philip feels up to writing some short stories, he'll see about getting them into his paper. . . . Oh, yes, Philip'll be quite famous before we know where we are!'

Joan came in. She looked tired and peaky. She was very quiet.

'Phil's ready for his tea, now,' she said.

'You're sure he hasn't been overdoing himself, darling?'

'No, I don't think so.' She scarcely regarded Victor. 'He painted for about twenty minutes. The rest of the time, I've been reading to him.'

Victor offered to take the tray for her. They all seemed a little surprised.

'You see,' Mrs. Lindsay explained, 'Philip's got so used to being waited on by Joan. We haven't told him you're here yet, even. Of course, you shall see him afterwards; when he's all ready.'

While Joan was gone, they discussed the later stages of the illness. The relapses. How the rheumatic fever had finally gone, but how delicate Philip was. He kept getting coughs and colds. When the weather really turned warm, they were all going away. Perhaps for the whole summer. Mrs. Lindsay thought it would be lovely if they could manage the Italian lakes. It was so necessary to keep him constantly amused. He mustn't be put out or crossed in the least thing.

Joan came back, and they had tea. But Victor noticed that she sat merely on the edge of her chair; restless. Presently, she said:

'Was that Phil's bell? I thought I heard it.'

And later:

'I'll just run and see if he wants anything more.'

At length, they proposed taking Victor to see him. Mrs. Lindsay led the way upstairs.

'Philip's got his own "studio," now,' she said, smiling. 'It used to be the box-room. He goes there in the afternoons, sometimes, and paints a little when he feels inclined. It makes a change from his sitting-room and his bed-room.'

The place was like a greenhouse. Small, and the gas-fire full on. There sat Philip, in a wheelchair, a plaid-rug muffled round his legs. The easel, with the picture of Joan – still in its very early stages – was put slightly aside to make room for a table with the tea-things. Philip wore a dressing-gown over his clothes. And, mittens. Currants, Victor was told, had made them.

He looked much as usual. Pale, but not noticeably ill. His chin was badly shaved, and he had grown side-whiskers and a thin dark moustache. He seemed in good spirits. They stood round while he talked. He was completely at his ease.

'Hullo, Victor. What have you been doing with yourself?'

They did not stay long. Currants remained behind, to read or chat.

'And you'll be sure to say, darling, the minute you feel tired. I think, in another half hour or so, you ought to go and lie down. You've had rather a longer day than usual.'

'How do you think he's looking?' Mrs. Lindsay asked, as soon as the door was closed.

'Take Victor down to Philip's sitting-room,' she said. 'He won't be using it again to-day.'

It was tidier than it used to be.

Joan apologized:

'Do you mind if you don't smoke? Phil's not allowed to, of course. And now he hates the smell of tobacco.'

He nodded. They sat down in silence, facing each other. She began to tap with her foot.

'Any news?'

'No. Nothing special.'

She smiled, yawned slightly and covered her mouth with her hand.

'Did you have decent weather?'

'Pretty rotten.'

'So was ours.'

She got up rather abruptly and sauntered to the window. Victor watched her a moment; rose also. He wandered about the room, examining the backs of the books on the shelf, hands in pockets. Fidgeting with the curtain-loops, she whistled a few bars, sharp.

'Had any tennis, lately?'

She seemed surprised that he should ask.

'No. Of course not.'

'Been to any shows?'

'My dear, I've scarcely stirred out of the house.'

He regarded her.

'It's about time you started then, we'll go to the Club a lot, this vac.'

She sighed.

'It would be nice . . . I mean, we will, sometimes – of course. But, you know, Phil still needs a great deal of looking after.'

'There's Mother, isn't there? And Currants. I don't see – '

His tone was a shade impatient. Or she was tired, peevish.

'It's special things to do with the nursing. I don't think you quite understand.'

'I'm sorry.'

'There's nothing to be sorry about.'

He had flushed. Her laugh was nervous. It ran on into:

'Such a screamingly funny thing happened last week.'

Only how none of them had been able to shake the thermometer down. And how Currants had suggested getting a block of ice from the fish-monger's, etc., etc. Joan kept giving the curtain little tugs to force out the emphasis. They were both laughing now. Each waiting for the other to stop first.

He asked the time.

'I must be pushing along, you know.'

'Oh, aren't you staying to supper?'

'I'm afraid I can't.'

'Having it with a lady friend?'

'Yes, rather.'

He was sheepish, unused to this sort of joke. She smiled. They smiled. Blood darkened his face slowly, heavily. He had just admitted to himself that he was vaguely, purposelessly eager to be gone from the house.

He asked:

'Has the specialist been again?'

'Yes. A few days ago.'

Her voice was rather deliberately casual. Her fingers drummed.

'Did he say anything definite?'

'No, not altogether. . .' She peeped out into the lamp-lit street. 'Except that it'll be a good long time. Phil's heart has been affected, you know.'

'Rotten luck.'

'He'll want looking after – for ages.'

Victor said nothing. He moved slightly; took a book out from the shelf, turned its leaves over, put it back. It was dark enough now to see this much reflected by the pane. She waited for him to speak until she could have yelled. Nothing happened.

She turned.

'I suppose you're going down to Surrey to-morrow?'

247

'No. My uncle's in Town. Wildlands is being sold.'

'Sold?'

'Yes. He's getting sick of England, he says. He's going up to the Orkneys for May. Then off on his travels again.'

'Really – how exciting.'

She felt absurdly tired, bored. This was what she told herself. She was trembling in the small of the back.

'Don't you wish you were going with him?'

She smiled; mocking, pale. Clenching the curtain-folds.

'He's asked me to. Several times.'

He was grave. She had never seen him so listless in manner. Her voice was false with animation:

'What a wonderful chance! And, by that time, of course, you'll have done with Cambridge for good?'

He nodded.

'So that, I mean, there isn't anything to stop you, is there?'

He made a slow movement. She could not wait for him, she went on:

'Where will he be going?'

'Oh. . . India, Malay, Australia, Brazil. I don't know for certain.'

248

'All round the world?'

'Pretty well.'

Her opal glittered in the light. She had been leaving it off a good deal lately. There were so many things always having to be washed. And now that she was wearing it again for the occasion, it seemed unfamiliar, pretentious. It didn't suit either of them. A ring suggests dates, plans, all sorts of bonds.

Hiding her hand from him in the curtain, she asked, smiling:

'I suppose he'll be away for a long time?'

'Oh, yes . . . for years.'

Five minutes later, with a joke about Philip's new medicine, she was closing the front door upon him. They were to meet again, of course, quite soon. She would have to see how Phil's cold went on. Victor was uncertain about his uncle's movements.

CHAPTER XIX

Next day, Philip was complaining that he never saw Allen. It was arranged that Joan should go round directly after lunch – this being a Sunday – and catch him before he went out.

Allen had been to the house several times lately. Mother never so much as tightened her lips. Since Philip's illness, (a period they all tacitly extended now by one day) visitors were only like the gramophone records they put on to amuse him. The Kreutzer Sonata. The Prince of Wales on Sportsmanship. Jazz. Anything for variety.

.   .   .   .

Allen was wearing a bow-tie.

'That's new, isn't it?' she asked.

He shook his head.

'But you don't wear one usually.'

'It's springtime.'

He grinned subtly. His suit, it occurred to her, was smart.

'You're perfectly sure that you hadn't some other engagement?'

'Nothing important. Nothing to compare with seeing Philip.'

His good-humoured irony; his faint, secret air

of pleasure explained itself. And – yes; basely, unreasonably, she minded. Jealous.

With what right?

We must have been much more lively then, because Phil didn't particularly object to the plan. Two of Allen's hospital friends, and three girls they brought. Right up the river, somewhere near Mapledurham. Mother was away from home. Currants never told her.

It was the punt-race which separated us. All in different boats. I wonder if anybody planned that?

And then it was getting quite dark, and there were Chinese lanterns. And a band playing, miles off, in some tea-gardens. I was rather tight on iced cider. Up against the bank, inside the willows.

Just look at the moon rising. It's like an arc-lamp.

It's like a phosphorescent melon.

A mospherescent phelon.

A phesphoroscent mollen.

Allen, you are an utter idiot, really. Don't. It hurts me to laugh. You'll upset the boat.

Here's a swan.

Hissing; it flattened, snaked its neck. Don't annoy it.

Come this side if you're frightened.

Our elbows touched. Suddenly flat sober. Still roaring with laughter. Where are the others?

We seem to have lost them.

Let's find them again. He pushed out at once.

We scarcely said another word to each other. Tearing into London at about half past three in the morning, crammed into somebody's car, singing and yelling like idiots.

I didn't meet him again for weeks.

Probably he's forgotten about it altogether.

.   .   .   .

Funnily enough, I'm nearly certain now that it's been ever since the evening Page came to my rooms. Leading down from that. Amazingly slowly, and with reactions. I suppose nothing serious could have survived that fight. The relief of being able to sit here and feel just selfishly pleased. Does it show in my face?

She looks better again to-day. Last time, I thought she'd be in bed by the end of the week. What a life in that house. Page ought to get her away from it.

I can just have tea there and then go on afterwards. Be there by six. Her mother would have-been there at tea time, probably; and her father, too. I'm glad I said that on Friday about coming late. I wonder what made me so nearly remark, after dinner: It's a peculiar thing. I'm invariably attracted by girls whose Christian names I loathe. Yours is worst but one. The worst is Joan.

I suppose one never quite gives anything up.

.　　.　　.　　.　　.　　.　　.

The 'bus had brought them to the corner, and, as they turned down Bellingham Gardens, Allen said, with a grin:

'Now for the Grand Levee.'

.　　.　　.　　.　　.　　.

She went straight upstairs to her room; although she scarcely admitted to herself, until she had pen and paper in her hands, what it was that she was about to write.

' . . . to tell you, at once, that I know I was perfectly vile, yesterday evening. I had a horrible headache, but that's no excuse. You were an angel not to chuck me up for good – and, as it is, you're probably sick of the sight of me. . . Oh, Victor, I really don't know what's been wrong with all of us, the last year. Yes, before Phil's illness, too, I mean. It was just the same. I feel we've always appeared to you as absolutely hateful people. I can't think what's made you put up with us for so long. But I do want you to believe that we have our better moments. . . . We must try and prove it to you. . . . Can't we make an entirely new start — imagine we've just got engaged all over again? And, look here, can't we get married quite soon? This summer? I don't know what you'll think of me for writing this, but I can't help it. . . .'

She didn't pause to re-read this, she had barely patience to scrawl the address. She hurried downstairs, out into the street. Liar. Coward. She began to run. No, she could never send it. Never. She ran faster. To have betrayed, on two sides of a piece of notepaper, everybody, everything. She was at the pillar-box. How utterly, ludicrously vile. The envelope crumpled in the slit. She thrust it through. It fell.

.   .   .   .

And then she was back in the basement, still out of breath, smiling as she hadn't smiled for months, giggling in the cook's face; she didn't care who noticed.

'Are you two ready for your tea?'

Philip was holding forth, in the best of humour, waving a mittened hand:

'You see, Allen, what I really dislike about your attitude is that it gets you nowhere. You refuse to venture, that's what it is. You're timid. Oh, I grant you one's got to have the nerve. . . .'